The Water of Life

The Water of Life

A JUNGIAN JOURNEY
THROUGH HAWAIIAN MYTH

Rita Knipe

with illustrations by
Dietrich Varez

University of Hawaii Press

Honolulu

Library of Congress Cataloging-in-Publication Data

Knipe, Rita, 1926–
    The water of life : a Jungian journey through Hawaiian myth / Rita
Knipe.
        p.   cm.
   Bibliography: p.
   Includes index.
   ISBN 0-8248-1242-5 (alk. paper)
   1. Mythology, Hawaiian. 2. Jung, C. G. (Carl Gustav), 1875–1961.
I. Title.
BL2620.H3K65   1989
299′.92—dc20
                                         89–5040
                                           CIP

For my own *ʻohana:* mother, sister,
children, grandchildren—and Bill,
who has been my companion on this
journey

The water of life is easily had:
everybody possesses it, though
without knowing its value.

C. G. Jung

CONTENTS

ILLUSTRATIONS

PREFACE

Mythology flows like a subterranean stream throughout Hawai'i. It has risen to the surface in numerous places on the Hawaiian Islands, often developing into local variations of basic mythological themes. Just as no body of water is more waterlike than any other, so too, no version of a myth is more "true" than another. To extend the analogy further, any individual expression of a mythic plot is determined by the color, size, and shape of the vessel used to dip it from the stream.

The mythic material contained within this book has been determined by my own position beside that stream. My standpoint is shaped by my personal and professional experiences. Often I have chosen a particular mythical variation because it best illustrates certain universal themes or Jungian concepts in the clearest, most economical manner. Other times, my selection is more emotional; I have a deeper response to some myths or versions of those myths than to others.

Some liberties have been taken with the mythic stories that were once part of the unwritten literature of Hawai'i. I have rewritten, edited, and summarized them, but always with total respect for their content and spirit. When citations have not been included, the material has been gathered from a number of sources, most of which may be found in the bibliography.

This book is a container that holds only a small portion of the fluid possibilities generated by an unknown universal source. Other people will find their own positions beside a waterway and provide their own containers. I agree with C. Kerényi when he states that "neither should we talk overmuch of 'sources'. The water must be fetched and drunk fresh from the spring if it is to flow through us and quicken our hidden mythological talents" (Jung and Kerényi 1963:1).

ACKNOWLEDGMENTS

My thanks to . . .

. . . Phyllis Charles and Susan Dunn for valuable suggestions and encouragement with the original manuscript;

. . . those who gave me unique assistance at the precise moment it was most needed: Yuklin Aluli, Jean Brady, Norma Gorst, Jim Iams, Ruth Iams, Marion Kagan, Victoria Nalani Kneubuhl, Carol Langner, and Dietrich Varez;

. . . my editor, Iris Wiley, who has earned my respect and appreciation with her sensitive skill;

. . . Bill Knipe for countless hours of support;

. . . the men, women, and children who have joined with me in my consultation room and have shared portions of their own journeys.

Mahalo!

1

Drumbeat, Heartbeat

My love affair with the Hawaiian Islands began when my left foot met the ground on the Big Island of Hawai'i. Like thousands of other people, I had fantasized for years about palm trees that swayed in harmony with tradewinds and warm waves that caressed gleaming, white sand beaches. Somewhere in the background of my fantasies, a dark, shadowy, masculine figure waited, promising passion, abandonment, and sensuous delights. Moonlight beckoned, blood roared; I would be transformed into a new life and identity.

With fantasies such as these, it was little wonder that I postponed an initial visit to the Islands. My more practical side had warned me to stay away from paradise. Rather than find disappointment in reality, I chose to keep the exotic images intact in my head as special territory that I could always visit in dull moments. The years had destroyed a number of technicolor fantasies and for a long time I held on to Hawai'i as a last paradisiacal outpost.

The actual experience was profoundly different from what I had fantasized or what I had feared. When my husband and I landed in Hilo, I placed one sandaled foot on the ground and was instantly aware of a definite beat. There was a pulse or drumbeat within the island itself that precisely matched the pulse inside my foot. Even through the shield of shoe leather, the beat demanded recognition. I turned to my husband and said, "I'm home."

For the next few weeks, I felt, saw, heard, tasted, and explored. Everything I touched was foreign, and yet familiar. The sense of familiarity was one I had never experienced before, as though I had known this place outside my personal life history. In many ways, Hawai'i is a mythical land; it offers a reality that encompasses numerous dimensions. I had never been here before, but in some inexplicable fashion, I recognized it immediately—which, of course, is what happens whenever we fall in love. And as a smitten lover, I returned to the mainland yearning endlessly for my beloved place.

While on Kaua'i during the same trip, I was introduced to Hawaiian mythology. My introduction came through the Menehune, the little people of Hawai'i, who were reported to have performed amazing feats, usually mysterious constructions of stonework only fragments of which remain today. As soon as we returned to the mainland, I began to read as many of the Hawaiian myths as I could find, exploring them within the context of Polynesian mythology as a whole.

I found myself deeply involved with a pantheon of unfamiliar deities with incomprehensible names, who inhabited a confusion of strange myths and legends. Gradually it began to occur to me that my fascination with those Polynesian stories had been activated by something within myself that was still hidden from me, something for which I yearned as if for an almost remembered place of origin. The Hawaiian bait lured me to become ever more firmly hooked because it held qualities that I needed to find within my own psyche.

The stories I read were emotional, sensual, explicitly sexual, poetic, and directly tied to the world of nature. They were, of course, translations of the original Hawaiian language and were in a form that the early Hawaiians had never used. Before the arrival of the New England missionaries, there was no written literature in Hawai'i; all cultural expression was communicated directly by chants, songs, hula, proverbs, and stories. As a result, what I was reading was a distilled version of other voices in other times. Nevertheless, I found a constant inner thread, which seemed to my unknowledgeable senses distinctly Hawaiian. What was most interesting to me was my own reaction, that of meeting an unfamiliar branch of a well-known family tree.

It would be more accurate to say that I had encountered a branch of the familiar family tree that expressed an aspect of the tree's roots for which I had yearned all of my life. I had longed for it without knowing what was missing or why I had been endlessly restless and unfulfilled. This branch, connected to those hidden roots, seemed to have something, and everything, to do with my reality as a woman.

So it has been first as a fascinated visitor and now as a resident of these Islands that I have continued to explore a stone age culture that nevertheless developed a complicated mythology and psychology. My exploration has led me beyond the myths, it has absorbed the very breath and spirit of the winds, waves, fragrances, flowers, dance, and music of the Hawaiian Islands. It has opened my heart to the people, the brown and golden Hawaiian people, who are changing now as they strive to reconnect with their own vanquished heritage.

More than all of this, it is a personal odyssey for me as I finally begin to uncover my roots as a woman, as though the very tradewinds blow my missing parts across my body and into my stomach, where they dwell while waiting discovery. There is magic here. It flies with the crimson feathers of tropical birds and it swirls in the foam of the ocean.

I have spent my life beside this ocean, first along the narrow strip of land which is Southern California and now on an island in the middle of the same ocean. Whenever I travel away from a coastal area, I begin to thirst with an inner dryness that is desertlike, as though my flesh has turned to parchment. Always, and perhaps in all ways, my soul needs constant contact with the water. *This is true for all of us, each in his or her own way.*

My first memories of joy are of days spent on the beach near Los Angeles. The beach seemed larger to me when I was a little girl. Not many grains of sand were needed to fill my hands with magic. I created fantasy dreams with a pail, shovel, wet sand, salty water, and with my own work, which was, of course, play. Playing alone, I had no sense of time. The flow of hours now seems like endless sun-sprayed grains of sand, slipping through my hands then, when I was very young.

Although that was more than half a century ago, I still have a deep connection with that four-year-old girl who spun herself into an island web and was absolutely isolated from everything but her imaginative play. My travels into the realm of fantasies, fairy tales, and creative adventures were in a direction which might be called *vertical* movement. By vertical I mean that most of my attention was focused upon a world that no one saw but me. In contrast, if I had chosen to play with other children at the beach (there must have been other children, although I do not remember them), my movement would have been in what might be termed a *horizontal* direction. Then my adventures would have been visible to others and would have taken place in what is commonly known as "the real world."

Vertical reality reaches up to the heavens where sky spirits dwell and it involves imaginative flights in pursuit of those spirits. Vertical movement also extends down to the earth spirits and into the darkness where the deepest roots of the human psyche are planted. We travel vertically when we pray, when we create, and when we dream.

Horizontal reality concerns the geographic dimension, the here-and-now of our senses, as well as much of our social and interpersonal relationships. It encompasses the territory of our practical daily activities. It focuses on shelter, food, sex, and on the various other necessities that keep our bodies and species alive.

All of us live our lives in both realms, vertical and horizontal, whether or not we are aware of the duality. An awareness of both realities as equally valid ways to experience our lives can bring surprising richness into commonplace events.

After moving to Hawai'i, I became increasingly aware of the duality of human travel and the relativity of human experience. Honolulu is a large city, but the island upon which it is built, O'ahu, is a small speck of land in the middle of the vastest ocean in the world. The Hawaiian Islands are farther away from a continental landmass than any other place on earth. Perhaps the very distance from a continent and the obvious geographic limitations of small islands brings a unique world view.

At first I was struck, as are most *malihini* (newcomers), by the different manner in which residents regard time and space. Having come from Los Angeles, with its endless interface of freeways, road systems, and far-flung communities, I was accustomed to driving long distances for short reasons. Suddenly I heard island dwellers complain about driving the few miles over the Pali, which divides Honolulu from Windward O'ahu. And yet, when money is available, these same people hop on airplanes and fly off to other islands or more distant places with remarkable ease, evidently viewing the many miles of ocean space as a minor inconvenience. Soon it became obvious that people here perceive miles and minutes in a way I had not encountered before.

As I adapted and adjusted, my own perceptions began to shift. Today a drive around the island is an adventure, and I have come to understand the reluctance to cross the Pali. Logically I am aware that the length of a mile has not changed, nor has the expanse of an hour, but an inner regulator has shrunk, or perhaps it has stretched, I am not sure which. Maybe, as was true during my childhood days on the beach, it now takes fewer grains of sand to fill my hands with magic.

On this Hawaiian beach, I turn away from the tall, concrete buildings, and I watch the waves. Space and time rearrange into a different pattern as I imagine long-gone foreign ships descending upon these once pristine shores. The ships are strange messengers, bringing change and devastation, as the past and future collide at the very place where I am standing. I imagine a drum, echoing from another time. If I had lived then, would I have been on a ship or on the shore? A scenario unfolds from the past:

A small group of New England missionaries, men and women, watch as more than a hundred Hawaiians dance and chant in the ancient ways of their ancestors. Despite the hot and humid tropical weather, the missionaries are covered with heavy clothing and heavier opinions. With self-righteous eyes, they watch the Hawaiians dance their hula and listen to what is, for them, barbaric noise. To the accompaniment of seemingly monotone chanting, thumping gourds and drums, and rattling dogs' tooth anklets, the dancers are honoring the strangers with their traditional welcoming dances.

The pale Calvinists, however, focus on ample brown flesh and what they see and describe in their journals as "shocking gestures, licentious behavior," and the Devil's own sinful seduction. The motes within the missionaries' eyes are formed by reflections of their own dark hell.

It was sometime in the early 1820s. The Calvinists had arrived on Hawaiian shores with the lofty purpose of saving lost souls. Several months earlier, the ancient Hawaiian religion had begun to crumble under the weight of foreign contact, and the missionaries lost no time in picking up the promising pieces of native culture, which they buried as deeply as possible in Christianity. Soon they put clothes on the "heathen bodies," taught Hawaiians how to read the words in the foreign Bible, and drove the hula underground or destroyed it altogether. The rigidly committed missionaries were incapable of understanding that their own world view was not necessarily divinely ordained, nor could they know that they had witnessed a celebration of sacred space when they watched the hula.

The Hawaiian culture had long been carried by traditional chants and dance. What seemed "lascivious" to the Calvinists, whose moral code was adopted later by numerous Hawaiians, was the heartbeat of the native people. It was an expression of their relationship to each other, fertility, nature, and their gods. The hula expressed their firm connection to the soul and source of their culture, individually as well as collectively.

Until the invasion of the white foreigners, all traditions, myths, legends, history, and literature were spoken. As a result, most articulated words had recognized *mana* (supernatural or divine power). Words once spoken became actual entities and caused changes in the world. The mana of words affected the physical, as well as the metaphysical world. For many Hawaiians, this is still true. A word is spoken with breath, which is spirit that moves what is uttered in a manner that can never be altered. Then, as now, the human body dancing the hula to chanted words is an expression of mana and an extension of the spirit that permeates the entire universe.

Even today, the chants, with or without accompanying dance, recount the history of the Hawaiian people and the domain of their gods. Although much of hula belongs to the everyday world of nature and relationships, it has an added spiritual quality. Spirit is found in nature, in human beings, and within the deities that populate the universe. It would seem that hula can become a ritual channeling of mana, a formalized bridge between the world of human beings and various planes of existence. The dancer's body seems to become an expression of the spirits of Hawai'i, both human and nonhuman, and it stirs a reflecting response within the spectators. I, who had never seen traditional hula before I came to Hawai'i, feel an excitement generated deep in my gut when hula is danced in such a spirit.

In hula, the dancers touch all of nature, including human nature, by finding the reflections within themselves. With basic steps and motions of arms and torso, they can portray the universe as they know it. The dancers' hands move downward, open to receive the breath of earth spirits, of the plant life that springs from the Mother of us all. The graceful hands receive and reflect ocean waves and surrounding mountains, swaying trees and flying birds. They reach above the dancers' shoulders to touch the heavens and the gods, and this realm, also, seems ritually channeled with body movements. The hula dancers may barely move from a small section of earth, and yet they express the entirety of the human condition as they know it, including their relationship to the divine.

Dance was the earliest way in which human beings connected with their gods. The ritual channeling of energy was understood to bridge the space between the dancers and the divine forces in the surrounding universe. It is possible that rituals, such as those of the dance, might still serve such a purpose for us today, and yet most of us do not dance and if we do, we rarely know how to move into sacred space, into the land of the gods.

During the current renaissance of Hawaiian culture, the hula is danced once more and the chants are heard again. As is inevitable, there are new ways to interpret the ancient patterns. The old and the new split apart, join for a while, and then separate again. Nevertheless, there is a similar spirit winding through all hula. That spirit is connected to the hula goddess, Laka, and it is powerful to behold, infusing the commonplace with sacred energy.

I understand the power of words and know too well the power of bodies, and so it is with apprehension that I put words about hula on paper. It is difficult to convey with pale syllables an experience, an image, which still dwells in the land of the gods and is eternal. How does one describe the incredible grace and fire of human beings whose bodies celebrate all of life? I have grown to love what I have witnessed, these scenes from another place, where the gods still live and move upon this earth.

Hula connected the people of old Hawai'i with the links of their traditions and to each other, proclaiming their inheritance as _kama'āina_, children of the land. The traditional hula patterns of words, beat, and dance have spanned the generations, although they suffered a long eclipse after white strangers first came to Hawaiian shores. Today hula is once again finding renewal of spirit after the devastation wrought by the foreigners.

Because the hula chants have carried Hawaiian traditions, as well as the links between generations, hula weaves a leitmotif through any discussion of Hawaiian mythology. Chants, hula, and _mele_ (songs) have become accompanying orchestration to my travels as I explore the local mythological realm. It is as though the distant hula drum gently beats in counterpoint to my thoughts. Moreover, that drum somehow conveys a vital power that has been lost from much of contemporary life.

> A question I ask of you:
> Where, pray, is the water of Kane?
> Yonder, at sea, on the ocean, . . .

There are other beaches now, white and golden sands that glow beside the surf. I pick up a conch shell or a rounded hard seed brought from another shore and I tuck them into a pocket or fling them back into the water. It makes little difference, whatever I choose to do with such a treasure belongs to the fabric of the day.

As I walk along the shores of this island or any of the jeweled Hawaiian Islands, I pace off territory that magically stretches in all directions. The point on the horizon where land and sky and water intersect becomes the center of the universe. Slowly the rich mythological atmosphere of this place begins to beat against the pulse in my feet and to touch me always again.

2

The Water of Kāne

A query, a question,
I put to you:
Where is the water of Kane?
At the Eastern Gate
Where the Sun comes in at Haehae;
There is the water of Kane.

A question I ask of you:
Where is the water of Kane?
Out there with the floating Sun,
Where the cloud-forms rest on Ocean's breast,
Uplifting their forms at Lehua;
There is the water of Kane.

One question I put to you:
Where is the water of Kane?
Yonder on mountain peak,
On the ridges steep,
In the valleys deep,
Where the rivers sweep;
There is the water of Kane.

A question I ask of you:
Where, pray, is the water of Kane?
Yonder, at sea, on the ocean,
In the driving rain,
In the heavenly bow,
In the piled-up mist-wraith,
In the blood-red rainfall,
In the ghost-pale cloud-form;
There is the water of Kane.

One question I put to you:
Where, where is the water of Kane?
Deep in the ground, in the gushing spring,
In the ducts of Kane and Loa [Kanaloa],
A well-spring of water, to quaff,
A water of magic power—
The water of life!
Life! O give us this life!

(Emerson 1964:257–259)

THE WATER OF KANE has been called the most beautiful chant in all of Polynesia. An ancient Hawaiian hula chant, it is a profound expression of a truth within us all, singing from the deepest reaches of the human soul. On the surface of the chant, we are informed that the sacred water lies somewhere in the land of the gods. The water is under the waves and beyond the horizon, in the heavy clouds supporting arches of heaven, somewhere on a floating island that periodically appears off the coast, or somewhere in the driving sheets of rain. Other stories and chants describe the water as hidden deep within a pit. Wherever it may be located, the water of life is under the protection of the god Kāne, and when a human being manages to secure it some of Kāne's power becomes available for human purposes. The sick who drink of it become healthy, and the dead are restored to life when sprinkled with its precious drops.

Most often Kāne is regarded as the leading god in Hawai'i. He is the ruler of procreation and life, holding within his domain the waters of healing, rebirth, and resurrection. Kāne's powerful water is known throughout Polynesia. The words of the chants may differ slightly, but the concept is the same. As an example, the New Zealand Maori say, "When the moon dies, she goes to the living water of Tane [Kāne], to the water which can restore all to life, even the moon to the path of the sky." The moon, when wasted and waning in its monthly cycle, bathes in the magic waters and then emerges each month as a new moon, freshly filled with growing strength. It is a miracle for all to witness.

Not only in Polynesia, but also throughout the world and during thousands of years of human history, people have spoken of the same water of life. The search for its healing powers is told in countless stories wherein the hero or heroine seeks its miraculous properties. Sometimes the water heals the sick; in other tales the water is needed to bring bloom again to a wasteland or to give the hero everlasting youth. The water is contained in a faraway pool, well, spring, river, lake, or grail, and the search for its blessings inevitably involves risk and heroic adventures.

One of the most ancient examples of the sacred water's healing properties is found in the Babylonian myth of Ishtar, who descended into the underworld of death, seeking to restore her son-lover, Tammuz, with the living water. Before she could return to the upper world, she, too, had to be sprinkled with the water of life.

Ancient Hawaiian mythology contains numerous references to such life-giving water. An example of a quest for it is found in the legend of Aukele.

> The heroic Aukele was the youngest of eleven sons. He was persecuted by his older brothers because he was their father's favorite and, as a result, had become their father's heir. The ten older brothers tormented Aukele unmercifully and were determined to kill him.
>
> Aukele was able to survive his brothers' various attempts at murder, until finally the brothers themselves died because of their rash stupidity. Now Aukele showed his heroic mettle. Despite his brothers' malicious behavior, he embarked upon a search for the water of life so that he could bring them back from the land of death. He traveled far to the eastern horizon, flying straight toward the rising sun. There, at the far eastern edge of the world, Aukele flew down into the pit of the sun, defying by sorcery the perils of death and escaping with the sacred water. The story of his many adventures is long and complicated, but he is best known as the hero who journeyed to the eastern pit of the sun for the water of life (adapted from Beckwith 1970).

Interestingly, it was Aukele's wife, a goddess, who gave him both the instructions and the magic with which to secure the water. And when he let the water slip through his fingers, she saved the last few drops and used them to bring his relatives back to life. Most often there is obvious feminine symbolism associated with the water of life, especially in regard to its container.

Various expressions of baptism and rebirth are associated with the same symbolism, as is the biblical well of living water in the Song of Songs. It is possible that the miraculous manna which fell upon the Israelites as they crossed the desert is a variation of the same theme.

In Hawai'i, the water of Kāne is an important element in transformative and healing rituals. Although traditionally sea or salted water, and even coconut water, have been used in such rituals, it appears that Kāne's water was always fresh, found in life-giving rain and streams.

There are thousands of rituals which use water as an instrument of healing and rebirth. Stories about the water of life, the search for it and its restorative qualities, are so numerous and universal that they clearly portray an elemental pattern that is common for all people in all times. It is a communal myth, shared by everyone.

The manner in which human beings are born from the maternal waters of the womb no doubt accounts for the universality of the symbolism. All of us are born from a watery womb, and by symbolic extension the feminine principle itself is the element from which birth and rebirth occur. As the water leaves our bodies when we die, so too the absence of water implies a death of some sort. The death may be a physical one or it may occur on another level.

As is expressed in the chant, Kāne's gift of water is found throughout the universe. Without it, no plant, animal, or human being can survive. Water is the most essential ingredient for the continuation of life, and such knowledge is shared universally.

Various other communal motifs and images appear with amazing frequency throughout the world and the history of mankind. They are found in individuals and in entire cultures. They are so faithfully and consistently repeated that they can be seen as basic to human nature itself. As with the search for the water of life, these motifs seem to have their base in our bodily instinctual heritage, but are extended to include our emotional and psychological heritage as well. As such, they are instincts of the psyche. The manner in which numerous patterns or themes are experienced universally is too consistent to be coincidental.

These communal themes are of life and death, of love and birth and rebirth, of crossings, conflicts, and union. Among numerous others, they involve such universal figures as heroes, lovers, Great Mothers, Wise Fathers, and Fools. They speak of the orphaned and miraculous child, and of Father Sky and Mother Earth. Repeatedly these, and similar motifs, are found in our mythologies and in the stories of our lives.

Jungian (Analytical) Psychology, as developed by C. G. Jung, has shed additional light upon these patterns, which are called *archetypal* because they are universal. We do not know how such patterns are born anew within each of us, but we can observe them as they function in our lives. We repeat them in our basic behavior and express them in our religions and art forms. We discover them in our dreams and as the motivating force within various rituals. As a relevant example, they are frequent themes found in Hawaiian chants, hula, and myths.

Mythology is a storehouse of such archetypal motifs. The patterns are universal, and yet they are colored in different hues by the individual culture that transmits them. The mythology of Hawai'i has numerous similarities to those of other Polynesian groups, but it is distinctly Hawaiian and organically belongs to that place and those people. Because of the geographic isolation of the Hawaiian archipelago, basic Polynesian themes have evolved in a unique and highly refined manner. Unfortunately, during the years of domination by foreign and overbearing cultures, many aspects of Hawaiian tradition and mythology have been erased. Chants have been forgotten, dances have disappeared, and stories have faded from memory, while the gods have drifted far over the horizon.

Mythology was sacred to the early Hawaiians, as it was to the American Indians and to other ancient cultures. Myths and legends carried the souls of the people, and the death of myths meant the destruction of lives and spirit. There was a time, in certain early cultures, when a sick person might be healed when told the mythological stories of the people. These stories connected him or her with the life power, the mana, at the deepest level of existence. Such a connection brings healing.

A myth stands in relationship to a particular society in the same way that a dream relates to an individual person. A dream reveals important psychological truths about the dreamer; a myth expresses a psychological pattern that applies to the entire society and to humanity as a whole (Sanford 1974). Mythology is an expression of human beings' most profound truths. Its reality stems from a deeper level than our everyday and manifest perceptions. As Jung observed, "All myths of all peoples and nations teach important psychological truths" (1976:461).

Actual belief in the existence of the water of life led explorers like Ponce de Leon to the New World in search of its source, the spring of living water that was the Fountain of Youth. Until recently, it was natural to imagine that the water of life lay somewhere just beyond the limits of explored reality. People could intuit that somewhere else, not here in this familiar setting, the miracle of healing and rebirth might be found.

Now, however, most of our planet has been fully explored and defined by maps and descriptions. We know that the water of life and the fountain of everlasting youth have not been discovered beyond the tallest mountain or across the broadest sea. Rationally we understand that the sacred water dwells in the imagination of human beings, and yet the myth continues to be a force within the human psyche and to express itself in visions, legends, rituals, and dreams. (I use the word *psyche* in its original Greek meaning as pertaining to the soul or spirit.)

As a Jungian analyst, I have heard many examples of the search for the water of life as it is enacted in dreams.

> One woman dreamed that she was traveling in a desert. In the dream, she felt as though she had been in the hot, dry, desolate place for a long time. Exhausted, she traveled on and on, knowing that somewhere in the distance there was a clear lake where she might drink and bathe. The lake was her destination and although she did not understand why it was her goal, she knew that she must reach it or die.

This dream, and others of a similar theme, are individual experiences of that basic archetypal pattern. Today we can understand that the motif of searching for healing water is a psychological one, meaning that it has to do with finding a place of renewal within the psyche of each of us, as well as within whatever we want to call the spirit or soul shared by all human beings. Psychologically the quest for the water of life is another way to describe the inner search, the quest for the healing center within. It is the symbolic journey toward wholeness.

The woman in the dream had come to consult with me because she had run out of ways to solve what felt like an endless series of problems. Nothing was terribly wrong; her children were healthy, her marriage was tolerable, and she had a job for which she was well trained. But if nothing was obviously wrong, nothing was right either. To put the issue more clearly, nothing in her life seemed meaningful to her. The dream accurately portrayed her emotional condition: she felt as though she lived her days and nights in a desert, and she suffered an endless inner thirst. If she could reach that clear lake, drink deeply and bathe fully in the waters of her own soul, she would touch her own center and be as one reborn. Psychologically she had reached the end of her previous adjustment to her life's demands, and a new orientation was needed.

We would make a crucial mistake if we misunderstood the method of travel during such a symbolic journey. Most often, it is not appropriate to embark on the quest literally: to get a divorce, leave one's children, or even change jobs. Although there are times when such drastic action is appropriate, usually the intrinsic demand is for psychological change. Change does not necessarily involve actual bodily movement toward an outer goal or destination, although it might do so. Sometimes both inner *and* outer change is necessary. The ways in which we can move horizontally are obvious: travel to another city, visit friends, find a lover, clean the house, or buy a new car.

As mentioned before, movement may also be toward an inner goal and then the process is vertical. The woman who dreamed about the distant clear lake needed to understand that her life seemed arid because her psychological ground, meaning her subjective reality, had not been watered for a long time, perhaps never. She had lived her life according to collective rules of "oughts" and "shoulds" and had not questioned them. Her reality as a woman was submerged in the feminine waters of the faraway lake and could be reached only within herself.

When the journey's destination calls for inner or vertical movement, little of the process may be revealed to the outer world. The traveler may sit quietly and cry, meditate, or even pray. He or she may wait for the first drop of emotional moisture to quench the dryness of despair. The difference between horizontal and vertical movement is one of perspective and, as must be obvious, they often overlap in actual life situations.

When the woman discussed previously began to touch the living waters within herself, her outer life changed considerably. She left her secure, but unchallenging, job and channeled her newly found energy and self-confidence into more satisfying work. As she was questioning her former collective rules of "oughts" and "shoulds," they began to dissolve and were replaced with appropriate responses to specific situations. Then all of her relationships, especially those with her husband and children, became more spontaneous and increasingly authentic. Such changes and shifts may be subtle and slow, but they are ongoing when our inner and outer experiences intertwine and influence each other.

These two directional realities, horizontal and vertical, are an integral part of traditional Hawaiian experiences. The duality is expressed in countless tales, proverbs, chants, and rituals. Hawaiians perceived the depths of their existence, and such awareness was reflected in their language, which was filled with allegory and metaphor. The *kaona* was, and still is, the secret core or seed beneath the surface of obvious meanings. It is the hidden meaning, the elusive treasure buried deeply in their oral traditions and literature. The existence of the kaona in words and phrases brings added enjoyment to Hawaiian life.

The Water of Kane provides one example. On a literal level, the chant relates to the planters' need for water to bring their crops to harvest. People who live close to the land understand how dependent life is upon fresh water and sunlight, which in Hawai'i means the water of Kāne. But the Hawaiians, searching for hidden meanings, would dig deeper. Ha'eha'e, in the first verse of the chant, is the Eastern Gate, where the sun brings each new dawn to the easternmost spot in Hawai'i. Ha'eha'e is also understood as the Eastern Gate of Heaven, and as such, it is a poetic, symbolic expression. Ha'eha'e implies more than a geographical place. In order to understand the Eastern Gate symbolically, we must encircle it with imagination.

Perhaps then we will think about the rising sun as an expression of the new day, the fresh light, and the dawning after the darkness of night. This might lead us to a perception of the Eastern Gate as the place of entry into a new dimension, the place where the light, as illumination, first appeared to the people. Kāne himself comes from the east; he is the god of life and new light. As we explore the image from various angles, we can begin to perceive the relationship between sunlight and human awareness. In the English language, we speak of *illumination*, which describes both light from an outer source, such as the sun, and an inner brightening where previously there had been the dark unknown. In the Hawaiian language, also, there are words, such as *ao*, which express both aspects of enlightenment.

Unless the chant initially came in a dream, the poet who first chanted of Ha'eha'e needed a way to express the gateway between nighttime and daylight, between knowing and not-knowing. As with all poets, he or she intuited something more than could be expressed with a factual description. Circling around the mysterious something, metaphors and unbidden images must have entered the poet's mind, and previously separated elements must have come together in new patterns. As long as the mystery, which is the undefined seed of Something, remains hidden, a symbol is a beckoning treasure that is alive, speaking to us in a lively manner whether or not we are poets. Words and images experienced symbolically do more than touch our heads and become one more idea to shoulder. They also touch our hearts. The appropriate way to approach the hidden treasure, the kaona, is in a circular manner, because lineal directedness buries the seed in gray sand and wrings all meanings from its potential.

A fuller understanding of the ways of an ancient people, such as the Hawaiians, can clarify our own basic patterns. The search for the water of life is such a basic pattern and the kaona within that pattern is the treasure.

Where flows the water of Kāne?

There are early Hawaiian myths and chants that describe the paradisiacal lands of the gods. Often these lands are on hidden islands, which Kāne controls and where he lives. The islands lie off the coasts of the main Hawaiian Islands. Periodically they are visible, but usually they are hidden from the people. Sometimes the myths describe the water of life as located on one of these sacred islands.

On one such island, there is a spring called Ka-wai-ola-a-Kāne (The-water-of-life-of-Kāne). The clear spring brings water and fish into a central pond by way of three outlets. One outlet is for Kāne. The other two outlets are for the gods Kū and Lono. The fourth major god, Kanaloa, is not mentioned in this myth, although he lives on an island with Kāne. The four great gods, Kāne, Kū, Lono, and Kanaloa, were the grand quaternity who towered above the land as primary deities of early Hawaiian religion, and they are still relevant today. Each of these gods has numerous forms, the different aspects indicated by the epithets attached to each name. As an example, Kāne-hekili means "thunder Kāne."

As discussed above, Kāne is the keeper of water, and thus of human life. There are numerous stories wherein he travels to various spots throughout the islands and thrusts his staff in the ground, causing water to gush forth. The springs so uncovered still bubble from underground sources today, bringing water to Hawai'i.

Images of island paradises, such as the one holding the water of life, are found everywhere in the world, not just in island cultures. My own fantasies about Hawai'i are illustrative of the lure such paradisiacal places have for a vast number of people. The yearning for a lost or hidden paradise undoubtedly has a connection to our personal histories. We have all been exiled from the safety of the maternal womb, a birth trauma that is shared universally. In a parallel trauma, most of us are in exile from the family womb of childhood. In addition, we are all exiled from an earlier form of human experience wherein people were contained in the greater womb of Mother Nature. The desire for paradise has further significance; it may also express a yearning for wholeness, implying a personal contact with transpersonal powers. That yearning for wholeness is the intrinsic motivation leading us to search for the metaphoric water of life.

In many mythologies there are islands of the blessed, which are often situated in the west, near the location of sunsets. In Greek mythology, Cronos, the grandfather of Greek gods, still lives on a magic island where a golden age continues forever. The Greek Elysium, as the dwelling place of those made immortal by the gods, is such a paradise, as is the Isle of Avalon in Celtic mythology, where King Arthur and other heroes went after death. Similar images are found in the mythical island continent of Atlantis and in the numerous other legendary islands discovered in oceans, and then somehow lost again.

The concept of paradise is frequently expressed in images of a garden, and evidently many ancient people portrayed the paradisiacal garden of the gods as still existing on an island, which was further to be understood as a gathering place of souls. In Polynesia, the image sometimes included various numbers of overworlds or middle lands between heaven and this earth, where we live. Inasmuch as this perspective also included an underworld, vertical travel was a natural way in which to imagine movement of the spirits (Beckwith 1970; Andersen 1969).

In Hawai'i, the legendary Kahiki is the actual name for Tahiti, but it often has additional mythological symbolism as the original home of the gods. As such it is frequently mentioned as the fabled place of origin, the paradisiacal homeland described in

numerous Hawaiian myths and chants. Although it is historically true that waves of Polynesian pioneers traveled to Hawai'i
from Tahiti, it is also mythologically true that Kahiki is one of
the names given to the faraway place where life began. Whether
creation occurred in Kahiki or on one of the floating islands, the
symbolic quality of the place is of paradise.

Undoubtedly it would have astonished the Calvinist missionaries if they had noticed the resemblances between the paradisiacal islands of the Hawaiians (which in myth often included a
magical tree of life and death) and the equally paradisiacal Garden of Eden. It is likely that the missionaries had a particular
tunnel vision that prevented them from observing such parallels.
All of us, even the most well meaning, are only able to perceive
reality from within the limits of our own vision. Too often we
defend our limited position and perception by negating the gods
of other people. We rarely ask: "And what archetypal images
move you?" "Or me?" "Am I blind to your godhead?" Perhaps
the best achievement we can hope for is an attitude which
acknowledges that yours or mine or theirs is but one of many
possible ways we can experience our mutual universe.

Our limitations of perception serve to isolate us on another
sort of island. Not all islands are paradisiacal, some resemble
prisons. In actual fact, an island is a geographical body of land
surrounded by water. The word *isolation* comes from the Latin
insula, which means island. It is possible to live on a small body
of land and to feel isolated by the magnitude of the surrounding
water. An island has a figurative, as well as a literal meaning, and
in this sense, we all live on small islands of awareness. From
such a limited position, we must make our peace with our fates.
Our psychological islands are situated in the middle of the largest
ocean in the universe, which may be imaged as the water of
unconsciousness. By definition, the word *un-conscious* implies
aspects of ourselves and our world of which we are unaware.

When we feel isolated on our small metaphoric islands, we
usually attempt to ease the discomfort through horizontal movement. We might actually travel somewhere else, and that solution might make us feel better, at least for a while. The woman
who dreamed of traveling in the desert had spent several years in
a flurry of travel plans and disappointing trips before she finally
looked for answers in another direction. Some people reach out
to friends and become busy with a distracting round of social
activities. Still others look for escape in more destructive direc-

tions, such as excessive use of food, alcohol, drugs, or any one of a variety of compulsive behavior patterns.

There are those who find their answers within the doctrines of organized religions or groups, but such a collective solution is not satisfactory for numerous others. Many of us have remarkably few outer resources that satisfy our restless quest for something more, somehow better, someplace else. What we do have, if we know how to reach it, is an inner source that can guide us to the wellsprings within our own psyches.

Recently a man shared a dream with me that illustrates a possible solution to the problem of psychological isolation. He felt himself to be stuck in a dreary job that was too limited for his potential and in a marriage that seemed monotonous. As is true for many of us, his "stuckness" was in direct relationship to his too narrow perspective. Every time he had an opportunity to make a change in his life situation, he felt overwhelmed and defenseless. His inability to make vital choices about his life had isolated him on a well-defended island, and he felt increasingly imprisoned by his own fears and the monotony of his days. As the man began to see himself and his problems in broader terms, he had an instructive dream:

> I dreamed I was in bed in my actual house. I woke up (within the dream) and noticed that it was extremely early in the morning. I felt rested and got dressed, ready to get my day started. This was strange because I'd gone to sleep late last night and I've been chronically tired for months. A dark man was with me, no one I actually know, and he was almost invisible.
>
> There was a large wooden square board in front of me, upon which a map of Oʻahu (where he lives) appeared. Suddenly the wooden board became enormous and was high above me, as if it was up in the sky. The map of Oʻahu had changed. Now there were shining lights on the board, some of which were larger and brighter than others. I realized that these represented population centers. The dark man told me that this was the best way to look at the island. He said that I can get a better perspective from such an angle and that I'll be able to see that the places also look like shiny crystals.

The man's dream informed him that his perspective of the psychological island upon which he lives is the important factor in his life situation. Viewed from a close and familiar perspective, his island is small and ordinary. When the island is seen vertically, however, it becomes a luminous place that begins to resemble the paradisiacal island that might hold the living waters of his life. As the dream suggested, its message came to the dreamer as a new awakening.

The new perception of the island presented the man with an image of a central archetypal force within him and within us all. It is an expression of wholeness, one of many possible images symbolizing the regulating center of our personalities. The man's dream gave him a dramatic view of the force that directs his life and his own inner population. It portrays one image of the goal toward which we all move, whether or not we are aware of its presence. There, in an inward direction, the water of life always waits. If we are able to widen our perspective and envision a deeper (or higher) reality, we can know that it is here, in this innermost space, that the spirit moves and can touch us, and a mysterious constellation of crystals eternally shines.

Now, in the age of Aquarius, the astrological water bearer, the quest for the water of life has become a communal myth of urgency. In too many ways, our lives have become barren and meaningless. Tidal waves of terrorism and chaos threaten our shorelines and swamp the land, flooding our ground without fertilizing it. When swamped by the water, we are overwhelmed, but remain in a sterile place. The gods, as well as the goddesses, have vanished below the surface of the ocean and beyond the waves on the horizon. We are drowning, but have nothing to drink. The floating islands no longer approach these, or any other shores.

Although the myth is a communal one, each of us must look within for the gods, the goddesses, and the healing water. And when we taste a drop of the living water of the psyche, which means the essence of our own souls, we are moved to travel always deeper, searching for another, and yet another precious drop from the everflowing spring or pool. Whoever is led by thirst to that water may drink. Those of us who thirst are the link between that pool and that spring. *We* are the link, the bridge; there is no other.

> A well-spring of water, to quaff
> A water of magic power—
> The water of life!
> Life! O give us this life!

3

Roots Planted in Darkness

Sᴇᴠᴇʀᴀʟ years ago I had a dream. It came at a time when I was struggling with a serious conflict. My emotions were raw, as though I were being torn apart by horses galloping in opposite directions, and my body reflected my distress in a strange crop of physical symptoms. Even worse, I felt as though I had lost an important connection with the inner balance that serves to keep me on course.

In the dream, I was aware of the conflict and the sense of disconnectedness, and also of the tensions that were manifesting in my body, so I went to a doctor's office for help. After several vague procedures, a young woman gave me the laboratory results. They were written in poetic form (which is the sort of unexpected twist a dream plot often takes). The diagnosis had to do with twos and pairs and conflicting opposites of various elements. I was advised that although the conflict appeared to be in my outer life, I would find the correct path and solution only within my own inner world. The surprising end to the dream prescription was that I was told to look to my 'aumākua for answers and assistance.

'Aumākua. The word startled me while I was still dreaming and was more of a jolt when I recorded it in my journal the next morning. The 'aumākua are the guardian spirits or ancestral gods of the Hawaiians. They are "selected spirits from among the dead who, because of their achievements or special qualities during life, are deified after death and transfigured into gods" (Kanahele 1986:81). They are both male and female and often appear in animal, plant, or mineral form. In the same manner in which family members share common ancestors, they also share common 'aumākua, which join the individual members together spiritually.

The 'aumākua can act as messengers, carrying the prayers of the Hawaiians to the more powerful *akua*, who are the gods of all the people and are imaged as being much farther away from everyday life. The 'aumākua are constantly present, and it is possible to have daily communication with them. They bring gifts to the people, including dreams, visions, and healing. Until recently Hawaiians believed that the 'aumākua brought dreams to them at night, and that they were the spiritual powers to turn to for the solutions to various problems. Many Hawaiians still have an underlying faith in the power of their ancestral spirits (Pukui, Haertig, and Lee 1972).

Inasmuch as I am not Hawaiian and was raised in a totally different culture, I was amazed to discover that I, too, might have helpful 'aumākua. I wondered how I, as a permanent but uninvited guest of Hawai'i, might approach the guardian gods of the people of this land.

Now I understand the dream's message much better than when I dreamed it, but the relevancy of the 'aumākua to my life is one of those mysteries that unfolds gradually, perhaps taking many years before all of its meanings are clear. Nevertheless, it is possible that at the moment of the dream, the 'aumākua had particular significance for me because they appear in multiple forms within nature, and thus are interwoven continuously with daily experiences. They act as a link to ancestral roots, and thus transcend time and space. They provide an expression of wholeness, which is considerably more than our conscious personalities.

In common with people of other early cultures, the Hawaiians took their dreams seriously. They believed that dreams were usually caused by the travels of the dreamer's spirit or by messages from the night, from *pō*, brought by the ancestor gods, the 'aumākua. The Hawaiians had no word, as such, for the unconscious psyche. However, among other meanings, the word *pō* implies night, darkness, eternity, and the realm of the gods. Because the concept of Pō shares so many characteristics with what modern psychology terms the "unconscious psyche," I have chosen to understand it as another way to perceive the same dynamics.

In regard to my dream, perhaps the main message was a reminder that conflicts in my outer life are usually reflections of the struggles in my inner space, most frequently fought between parts of myself that I have not yet claimed. As is true for all of us, problems that seem to be occurring in outer reality often are extensions of an internal drama. At the moment of my dream, I needed a reminder of that truth. No matter how many times we learn this lesson, we must realize it again daily. And if we forget, our nighttime dreams will present us with new instruction.

As previously stated, there seems to be a center within each of us that sends messages our way, often in the form of dreams, but also as visions, myths, creative images, and other symbols. Indeed, the language of this central force often expresses itself symbolically. In the previous chapter, there was an image of such a center, seen as a constellation of crystals in the man's dream. The center may be called many names, such as God, a reflection of God, gods or goddesses, Great Spirit, or a higher self. Jung referred to this transpersonal power as the Self.

The name is a matter of minor significance, but the central force itself is all important. The Self includes our conscious and unconscious personalities and it is also the center of our totality. As in the Chinese concept of Tao, it is an expression of the duality and union of such opposites as light and dark, male and female, positive and negative, and the masculine and feminine principles of *yang* and *yin*. It contains the seeds of our true potential as individuals and is the teacher and guide which would lead us ever onward to a fuller expression of our evolving uniqueness as human beings.

Our conscious personalities are like small, limited islands of isolation. In early childhood, these islands of our personal reality break the surface of the unconscious waters from which we are born. As we develop chronologically, the islands grow in size, but remain limited by the perspective of our egos. We live on these tiny ego islands, safe from the dangers of swirling tides, but dependent upon the waters for nourishment and revitalization. The vast ocean surrounding us all is a metaphor for what Jung termed the *collective unconscious*, meaning that it is at the deepest level of the psyche and is shared by all human beings. All of the archetypes are rooted in the collective unconscious, here imaged as a vast ocean. Individually and collectively we have been born from that ocean, as if from a dark, watery womb, a psychological process that is beautifully expressed in the poetic images of the Hawaiian creation chant, the *Kumulipo*.

Kumulipo means "beginning-in-deep-darkness" or in the far past: *kumu*, the source, planted in Pō, the darkness of the past. The deep darkness of Pō is the world of the spirits, of the

unknown forces which still exist within the dark psyche of each of us. It is both a communal darkness and an individual darkness. As is the case with all psychological and mythological truths, it is likely that the *Kumulipo* was created by intuition and inspiration, and not as an intellectually thought-out thesis. For this reason, it is valuable to explore the chant as an expression of life as it truly is. There are several major translations of the *Kumulipo*. The following information is culled from the translation and commentary by Martha Beckwith.

The creation chant consists of more than two thousand lines and is divided into two periods. The first period is that of Pō, or Darkness, and the second part is that of Ao, or Light. The chant is said to have been composed around the year 1700 for the birth of a chief, although the first section appears to be considerably more ancient. Evidently this chant was recited by two *kāhuna* (priests) to honor Captain James Cook when he landed in Hawai'i.

The chanted imagery is exquisitely precise. After an introductory song:

> The night gave birth
> Born was Kumulipo in the night, a male
> Born was Po'ele [the darkness] in the night, a female
> Born was the coral polyp, born was the coral, came forth
> Born was the grub that digs and heaps up the earth, came forth

In the following lines, all known Hawaiian species of plant and animal are born, male and female each: *Man for the narrow stream, woman for the broad stream*, clearly sexual imagery and thus creative and creating of life.

> The long night slips along
> Fruitful, very fruitful
> Spreading here, spreading there
> Spreading this way, spreading that way
> Propping up earth, holding up sky
> The time passes, this night of Kumulipo
>   Still it is night.
>   (Beckwith 1972)

The images of this creative process, evolving from the dark source, wherein the males grow strong and powerful while the females receive and conceive, continue until the birth of the new human being. These were sacred chants and the kāhuna who recited them knew the entire length of birthings with exact wording and inflection. Such memory feats were the necessary means of transmitting the traditions from generation to generation.

Only at the end of a long series of male and female births is the human being created. Ao, the Day, is reached, bringing human consciousness, when both humans and gods appear in the light. It is also understood that the gods live in Pō, but are unseen. The gods need human beings to recognize the divine spirit, and then it is light. The origin of the light of consciousness, however, lies with the source, which is also the beginning.

Beckwith says that there is no doubt that the first period of the chant, the Pō, is a reworking from ancient material. There are similarities to the creation chants found in various other Polynesian groups, many of which also describe the evolution of life from a watery source. Therefore, we must view the *Kumulipo* as an important expression of early Hawaiian culture. As with *The Water of Kane*, the *Kumulipo* expresses a universal truth.

The latter period of the chant, from the dawn of light to the birth of the new chief, is designed to give the genealogical history of the child's ancestors. Mythological accounts of male and female deities are followed by another long list, this time of the chiefs, both male and female. The list of chiefs is of interest historically and as an indicator of each chief's vertical ascent (or descent) from the rooted source and the time of the gods, thus indicating the divine inheritance of the chiefs and the concentration of mana with which each was born.

The *Kumulipo* is a brilliant poetic expression of biological and psychological creation. It is a patterned mixture of inner and outer facts, with a current of emotional charge woven into the fabric. It sings of humankind's intimate relationship with all of nature. This was the world view of early Hawaiians, who knew that they were an integral part of a vast natural field. The chanted imagery pulls together threads found throughout the universe and expresses the duality of life: dark and light, male and female, plant and animal, above and below, ocean and land—all possible opposites of Hawaiian experience perceived as dualities. The Hawaiian perception of life, like that of other Polynesians, includes an appreciation of the dualistic nature of existence.

My own dream, wherein the conflicting pairs of opposites were part of the diagnosis, is an individual experience related to the same theme. At the time of the dream, my frame of reference was altogether too one-sided, and the diagnosis suggested a more holistic perspective. The poetic nurse informed me that the solution lay within, in the place where the opposing forces might be united in a creative, new perspective. This, too, is a form of human creation. Dreams that resemble various creation myths are common when a new psychological attitude is needed and there is a possibility of its birth.

The *Kumulipo*'s emotional charge must be understood as both sexual and symbolic and, ultimately, as the element that unites the sexual and symbolic. Factors which the Western moralist might perceive as irreconcilable opposites, such as sexual and symbolic, are here unified as a basic duality. The same duality is expressed in hula chants and dances, such as those that celebrated the birth of a new chief and included words and gestures in praise of the royal genitals. The next generations of divine royalty would issue from the genitalia of the little chief, reason enough to celebrate its size and mana.

The kaona hidden in songs and stories is as often a sexual allusion as it is a symbolic one. Frequently it is both sexual and symbolic, which is a dualistic expression of the fullness of life. In numerous chants and myths of Hawai'i, one sees how deeply the emotion of creativeness and the emotion of sexuality are intertwined and have a common root.

Evidently precontact Hawaiians experienced sex as natural, fun, and extremely pleasurable. They were trained from childhood in ways to give and receive as much sexual enjoyment as possible. The foreigners brought sexual diseases and missionary morality with them, along with the polarization between the sexual and the sacred, and soon the Hawaiians themselves began to suffer a division between parts of themselves. Today the extent of the split seems to depend upon the degree of cultural conflict within each individual Hawaiian or part-Hawaiian.

When we forget the common root shared by the sexual and symbolic (thus spiritual) aspects of life, we have a split within ourselves that leads to negative symptoms and unnecessary suffering. We can observe such a division in our daily lives when a misused or unused creative gift may result in sexual problems, or when sexual promiscuity, frigidity, or impotence may have a symbolic cause. Or when moralistic "shoulds" and "oughts" inhibit natural and appropriate sexual instincts. On the other hand, a greater awareness of the connections between sexuality, creativity, and creation greatly enriches our lives. Knowing that these human experiences are interconnected at a common root can help us differentiate one from another as they appear in our lives, and to decide upon the appropriate response in each instance.

The interplay of sexual and symbolic images is found in the majority of origin myths and myths of creation. The origin myth of the taro plant is an illustration. In old Hawai'i, taro was believed to be primordial and was, in fact, the staff of life. Myths and symbols surrounding this important plant are of special interest because they can reveal to us today some of the rich wisdom of the past. The mythological realities that disclose themselves to each generation are timeless, often needing only a seasonal watering to spring forth with life again. We can find such seeds whenever we harvest the fundamental food of a particular culture. Concurrent with the revitalization of Hawaiian identity and pride, there is renewed interest in the cultivation of taro. Taro is one of humankind's oldest food crops and was more highly cultivated in old Hawai'i than anywhere else in the world. One of the best-known Hawaiian myths is related to the origin of taro.

Wākea, the male ancestor of all Hawaiians, and Papa, the earth mother goddess, lived together as man and wife. A daughter was born to them who grew more beautiful with each moment of her life. Her name was Ho'ohoku-i-ka-lani, which may mean "The heavenly one who made the stars."

After a while, Wākea desired his daughter and wanted to make her his wife also. He was anxious not to arouse Papa's jealousy, so his kahuna suggested that *kapu* (taboo) nights be arranged wherein husbands and wives would sleep apart from each other. Thinking this a fine idea, Wākea told Papa of the kapu nights and she consented to the new arrangement. On those nights, Wākea secretly slept with his daughter. After one such night, Wākea overslept the awakening song of his kahuna and Papa discovered her husband in their daughter's bed. The husband and wife quarreled and subsequently separated from each other.

Ho'ohoku-i-ka-lani's first child by her father was born prematurely, almost in the shape of a root. Wākea buried the strange little body at the east corner of his house. Soon a taro plant grew from the burial place, and Wākea named it Hāloa-naka (long petiole or stalk).

Later, when a real child was born to Wākea and his daughter, Wākea named him after the older brother, the taro plant, and called him Hāloa. This second Hāloa became the direct ancestor of the Hawaiian people. Thus, in kinship terms, taro is the older brother and the senior branch of the family tree. Mankind belongs to the junior branch, stemming from the younger brother (adapted from Handy and Handy, with Pukui 1972; Beckwith 1972).

Papa is the original feminine principle, the Mother Earth. Hers is another name for Haumea, the earth goddess herself and the womb from which all is born. Wākea can be seen as the masculine principle, the Father, the progenitor, the light of day and the bright heavens, the Wide-Spread-Sky.

The symbolism related to Wākea, as well as to various other phallic gods, represents the fertilizing and generating masculine force found in all life as half of the creative process. The feminine principle, in various natural forms, which include Papa and Haumea as expressions of Mother Earth, is the necessary other ingredient for all creation.

At the beginning of the myth, Wākea and Papa are united, living in what appears to be absolute togetherness. In Polynesia, as in other parts of the world, creation myths often begin with the separation of the primal parents. Originally the first parents clasp each other in an unending circular symbiosis; the male and female elements are a single unit, with no space between them. In such a state, there is no movement and nothing can change. Wākea and Papa were separated by the birth of their daughter and Wākea's subsequent sexual involvement with her. As a result, there was space enough between the primal parents for new beginnings, of both plant life and human beings.

This universal theme is expressed in our personal psychology also. Only as we separate from an original unity with the forces of the unconscious, which is analogous to living in the paradise of a childhood existence, can we become increasingly differentiated and aware of ourselves as separate individuals. Anything that is in symbiotic unity with primal energy is unable to change or create. It simply is, static and essentially formless in its watery condition. The island has not yet emerged from the ocean, and human creation of any sort depends upon solid ground on which to stand.

Biologically we know that the creation of a new human life requires two separate entities to come together in union. The same is needed for psychological creation. The ego (on the island bearing our name) must be sufficiently emerged from the unconscious psyche to interact dynamically with it and bring forth new birth.

Such essential differentiation is expressed in the *Kumulipo* when names are given to the various plants and creatures as they are separated into pairs of opposites. There is a duality expressed, not only of male and female, but also of the creatures belonging to the sea and those of the land; these are born in pairs, in an alternating rhythm. From the dark chaos comes separation, differentiation, and creation. Once an element is given a name, it moves toward the light and becomes known.

In our lives, we experience such a separation initially as conflict. Symbiotic togetherness feels comfortable and secure for varying lengths of time. We are contained within the security of an "us" marriage or the closeness of a family unit, and we feel ourselves to be relatively safe from the dangers on the other side of the wall. We huddle together in a full circle, perhaps around a small domestic fire, while the noises of the teeming jungle are kept outside and often ignored.

Separation can begin with any one of a multitude of causal events, and when it starts, the situation becomes increasingly uncomfortable. We tumble out of the magic circle and must face both fire and jungle alone. It feels as though a once protective wall has crumbled. The growing child has nightmares or school phobia, the adolescent suffers constant trauma, and husband and wife view each other in a startlingly different way. They may quarrel or become estranged. We might wish it were otherwise, but only as a result of psychological separation, with its accompanying conflict and pain, are we able to experience the birth of a new beginning. Married couples, who have fallen into a symbiotic (and monotonous) coexistence, frequently describe that their most exciting sexual encounters have followed a stormy battle. Once again they are able to perceive each other as the "Other"—as unpredictable and stimulating.

We can conjecture that Wākea and Papa began to separate before their daughter was conceived, although she was the new element which totally divided the primal symbiosis. As in other such myths, mother Papa and daughter Hoʻohoku-i-ka-lani may be understood as two aspects of the same feminine principle: the older and the younger, each bearing within her womb the fruit of the past and the roots of the future. Hoʻohoku-i-ka-lani is the daughter of the earth and she is also the mother of what will be born next, which in this myth means both the staff of life and the people of Hawaiʻi. Inasmuch as her name implies that she made the stars, she may be understood as the mother of chiefs, because there was a direct connection between royalty and stars in Hawaiian thought. In similar myths in various cultures, mother and maiden are connected with the moon and its monthly cycles, from young to full, from old to dead, and then to rebirth endlessly.

In the taro myth, the kapu nights scheduled by the kahuna were dictated by the waxing and waning of the moon. According to at least one source, this was also the beginning of the various kapu that prevented women from eating with men and from eating certain foods (Pogue 1978:42–44). As a further example of the kapu system, in old Hawaiʻi taro could be planted, harvested, cooked, and prepared only by men; women were forbidden such tasks because of their menses.

The word *kapu* means a prohibition, but it also implies that which is sacred, holy, or consecrated. The kapu system in Hawaiʻi, as in various other parts of Polynesia, was rigidly enforced, between the chiefs and the commoners as well as between the sexes. It is clear that the numerous kapu surrounding women were infused with a strictness fed by fear, as though the women themselves, or some quality of the feminine principle, could unleash overpowering and dangerous forces.

It is interesting to speculate whether Papa, and the females who were to follow her, were so empowered by their connections to the lunar forces (as expressed by their fertility and menses) that they had to be separated from the males, so that masculine (perhaps solar?) energy might become more potent.

If Papa and Hoʻohoku-i-ka-lani are considered two different aspects of the feminine principle, a difference in Wākea's relationship to them is apparent. Wākea and Papa were equal partners until Wākea desired their daughter. Then Papa was separated from him and her daughter became the husband's mate instead. But Wākea was also father to his daughter. It is likely that this dual relationship gave him additional power. When the omnipotent parental image is combined with that of the mate or spouse, it becomes enormously powerful, whether it is assumed by the mother with a son-lover or by the father espoused to his daughter. Wākea's marriage to his daughter, therefore, expresses a shift in balance, which would have given added strength to the patriarchal forces within the Hawaiian culture.

In Maori mythology, it was Tane (the Hawaiian Kāne) who separated the primal parents. Tane's fierce, powerful thrust tore the heavens from its embrace with Mother Earth, rending the parents apart so that darkness was made manifest and separated from light.

Kāne's great potency, as expressed in the chant *The Water of Kane*, is often associated with the cultivation of taro. Taro, bamboo, and sugarcane are identified with him, all of which have shoots that push up through our Mother Earth with phallic form and strength. Erect stones, called *pōhaku o Kāne* undoubtedly have the same symbolism, especially when they are near clear springs. These, however, were more often family altars (Handy and Handy, with Pukui 1972).

Kāne is also the god of sunlight. We look for Kāne's blessings at Ha'eha'e, the Eastern Gate of the Sun. As previously discussed, the rising sun symbolically implies a new birth and awakened consciousness. In the taro origin myth, the rootlike first child was buried at the eastern side of the house, followed by the emergence of the green shoot from that same place. It is likely that the new growth, appearing on the eastern side of the house, has much the same solar significance.

The dark soil, like the dark night and the shadowed ocean, all belong to the realm of the feminine element, whether we call her Papa, Haumea, or any of the names of the multitude of mother goddesses found in other cultures. The Great Mother, as an archetypal image, is the matrix of our origin as human beings and is best symbolized by her womb in its various forms. That womb holds the water surrounding the roots of all life and is found in the *Kumulipo* as first source. The Great Mother is found as the earth, the ocean, or as the all-powerful maternal element in a myriad of other forms and manifestations. Because we find her image reflected in the figures of our personal mothers, who are our first experiences of life, hers is the most powerful of all archetypal images, the one that often rules our fates.

She is Yin, the container that bears all life, which nourishes and then releases, only to embrace us again when life leaves our human forms. She is the night that gives birth to all creatures. She is the receptive feminine power that actualizes the masculine creative thrust. She is the darkness that opens to penetrating light and conceives, brings forth, and then closes again. And so we find the taro plant, symbolized as the child of the Earth herself, who has been fertilized by the masculine insemination of the heavenly progenitor, Wākea.

Throughout the history of our world, fertility, birth, and death have been associated with the universal forces that are ruled by the feminine or lunar powers. All of these also involve the resurrection of a plant that serves as the staff of life for a particular culture. In early Mexico, for example, the Maize God of the Cora Indians ritually sang the following song after the corn was given to the fire for transformation: "My younger brothers (mankind) appear but once. Do they not die forever? But I never die; I appear continually . . ." (Jung and Kerényi 1963:116).

There is a mythological, thus archetypal, connection between death and procreation that is often seen and experienced in the image of a plant as a renewing form of being. This association is also perceived in the phenomenon of the dying and returning moon. Symbolically the birth of a divine child, one such as Hāloa, is frequently associated with the newborn fruit of the Earth, who is his divine mother.

As previously stated, there are countless variations of Hawaiian myths, and no single version is the "correct" one. Often they can be seen as different amplifications of a single archetypal core. There is an ancient variation of the Wākea–Papa myth that clarifies more of its symbolic meaning.

Wākea is the God of Light, who looked down upon the earth and beheld the beauty of Papa-i-ka-Haumea, who is the same earth goddess as in the first version, but here identified by both of her names. Wākea fell in love with her and was filled with sorrow because he knew that he could never approach his beloved. The great flames of the sun, which surrounded him, would scorch and burn her if he drew too close to the earth. Wākea cursed his godhead, which made him ruler of the sun and master of light.

He cried in heaven for Kāne, the creator, and begged to be released from the tremendous task he had undertaken. Although

Kāne understood Wākea's sorrow, he refused to release the God of Light from his tasks.

Knowing that he would never be able to quench the thirst for his love, Wākea went to the God of Fertility and begged for a portion of that god's creative powers. When the power of fertility was given to him, Wākea combined it with the light of the hot solar flames surrounding him. Then he looked upon the head of Papa-i-ka-Haumea, and from his eyes he cast forth a beam of light that he had rendered fertile.

The light fell upon the earth goddess, and a girl-child, Ho'ohoku-i-ka-lani, was born from her head. When Wākea looked upon his daughter, he loved her also and he sent forth a beam of light that bathed her in his glory. As a result, she conceived within herself a man-child, who was born to be named Hāloa. Hā-loa means "He-of-the-long-breath." His name may also be translated as "He-of-the-long-spirit," because spirit is manifest in the breath of gods, as well as in the breath of human beings. Hā-loa also means "long life."

Hāloa lived for many generations, and it was he who first brought the Hawaiians to Kahiki, and then across the ocean to Hawai'i. There Hāloa erected a great temple in Waipi'o Valley to honor his divine father, Wākea, who had followed Hāloa across the ocean (adapted from Kapiikauinamoku 1956).

Evidently the taro plant also followed Hāloa to Hawai'i, where Waipi'o Valley on the Big Island provided an ancient and richly fertile home for its cultivation. Now we can begin to understand more of Hāloa's nature. Hāloa is both taro and man; he combines the fruit of the earth and the fruit of the heavens, because spirit is the breath of the gods. Hāloa is the elder brother who dies with each season, only to be born again eternally, and he is also the younger brother who lives but once and then dies forever. But the breath, the spirit, the *hā*, continues from generation to generation.

Symbolically the two brothers are branches growing from the same tree of life. The *Kumulipo* expresses this idea in another way. The dark source, kumu, meaning also "stem" or "stalk," gives birth to plant life, of which taro is a species, and also to animal life, to which human beings belong.

> The rootstalk grew forming nine leaves
> Upright it grew with dark leaves
> The sprout that shot forth leaves of high chiefs

> Born was Poʻeleʻele the male
> Lived with Pohaha a female
> The rootstalk sprouted
> The taro stalk grew.
>
> (Beckwith 1972:71)

Throughout the history of humankind, plants have come to symbolize human spiritual development. Wākea and Kāne, both gods of procreation, are mythological images for the fertilizing factor which begets the plant or brings new light to each sunrise. The plantlike meaning of life occurs in expressions of birth and within the mysteries of death and resurrection. The buried still-born first son was reborn as a taro plant. The second son, Hāloa, was born in the form of a human child, who would become the original ancestor and a symbol of all life on this earth.

Spiritual growth is like a plant, like taro, needing firm rooting in the earth, which is the ground of our human reality. Both human spirit and taro need constant nourishment from the living water of life. The sprout will send forth its leaves, as chanted in the *Kumulipo;* it will reach upward to the heavenly spirit, but only if the root is firmly held within the dark, moist earth, which is the womb of our basic nature. The soul emerges from the very ground upon which we live, and from where we are daily reborn. The spiral and cyclic manner in which the actual taro plant grows becomes a metaphor for spiritual, and thus psychological, growth. In such a manner, taro expresses the continuation of life, the bridge between generations, and the ancestral spirits who provide food and fruition.

It is likely that the early Hawaiians had an intuitive understanding of taro mythology in just such a symbolic way. *Poi* is a basic Hawaiian food, made of taro that has been cooked, pounded to a paste, and usually fermented. The calabash of poi was sacred to Hāloa, and to the presence of Kāne (Handy and Pukui 1972:115). The round calabash is a perfect image for the feminine womb, within which the arduously pounded taro is contained and then offered as the very staff of life. Because of its sacred nature, behavior in the presence of poi was strictly controlled, especially when the calabash cover was removed and the poi exposed. For was not the god himself present in the bowl?

The connection between taro and Hawaiian tradition is poetically expressed in the concept of ʻohana. ʻOhana is the basic family system, which is like the taro in that it springs forth from a single source, a common ancestor. *'Ohā* means the young taro growing from the older taro stem, and the added *na* makes it plural and signifies descendants from the same family stock, whether plant or human. Thus the staff of life is firmly connected with each particular family tree. Although the taro is harvested when ripened, the plant itself is reborn again and yet again when cuttings from the taro stem are broken off and replanted for the next season. The process can continue indefinitely. In a similar manner, family members may die, but as long as parts of the essential stem are planted and replanted to spread again, life continues.

In Hawai'i today, the close relationship between 'ohana members has broadened to include a strong bonding between members of the entire Hawaiian community. The revitalization of these interrelationships seems necessary to Hawaiians finding their common heritage as a people. Such ancestral connection and pride were stolen from them with the domination of their land, which for Hawaiians means the source from which they are born. The strengthening of their roots may serve to reconnect them with the 'aumākua spirits also, so that the root system will bring nourishment to their souls.

The need to find renewal and rebirth is equally urgent for those of us who are not Hawaiian. Most of us have lost our bearings. We have lost connection with our own life force and with the instinctual tie to the earth upon which we live. We have lost our relationship to the world of nature and to the world of the spirit, as well as our connections with each other. Our human nature is in jeopardy as we balance on the sheer cliff that is the terrain of contemporary life. Most of us have no social structure like an 'ohana to provide support, so we each must find our relationships with one another and with whatever we may call our 'aumākua.

The second myth illustrates a modern danger. Wākea, as the God of Light, personifies the heat of the sun. As is the case with all true symbols, the precise meaning of the sun here is impossible to define, although it appears to express extreme heat, as well as supreme light and power. As expressed in the myth, we, who are of necessity held by gravity to the earth, are in danger if we get too close to the sun. The unveiled, unhidden, glaring, golden eye of the godhead can burn and destroy us if we forget its power and our own vulnerability. We are children of the earth goddess, we are earthlings.

When we human beings, in arrogant hubris, believe that we are the masters of the universe and forget that we belong to this earth, then we can be destroyed by solar fire. The myth tells us that solar power must be combined with the spirit of fertility before any creation is possible. Those bright flames are more powerful than mortals, whether they are found on a burning bush on Mount Sinai, within a nuclear explosion, or in dangerous penetration of our planet's atmosphere. If we lose our humility before the gods, we may lose our earth. The ancient wisdom remains valid today.

Those of us who are separated from a support system, such as that of the 'ohana, often find it impossible to return to the structure of such a system. We cannot go back, we are undernourished in our present condition, and yet we have no guidelines to lead us into the future. Stuck, we are unable to reconnect with traditions that have lost their relevancy and vitality. We feel isolated and alienated, and have lost our way. Where now? This, too, is a modern collective experience, this alienation, and it seems to be connected to the shared search for the water of life. Primal Paradise is lost and so are we.

The terrible dilemma has an equally awesome answer. For most of us there is no established direction. There are no ancestral traditions to guide us on a pathway. We are forced into a dead end, where the only answers are unpredictable and individual. Those of us who have fallen out of a traditional support system must find our own way. Our central source, by whatever name, must be found anew by each of us, and there are messages that we alone might comprehend, if we learn to listen.

4

Enchanted
Reflections

Our only friend being our love for one another,
It is hooked and it bites to the very inside of the bones.
O my love, speak to me! . . .
When am I to be contented, O my love?
My love, O come back!
For love has again entered my heart,
For it pains me in my effort to withhold it,
My love, O my love, come back!

(Elbert 1959)

AH LOVE! In any language a love story stirs the blood and sings of the incredible longing for the beloved other. *Without you I am empty, forever yearning, trying to grasp yet again my own life, my own soul which awakens only in your presence. Ah, love, cleave to me that I may live.*

Falling in love is tantamount to walking with the gods and may be the nearest we living human beings can ever approach a heavenly space. Inevitably, of course, falling in love has its decidedly difficult moments when it seems like falling into a hellish pit. Whatever the outcome, falling in love is a happening which everyone needs to experience at least once, just so that we can feel ourselves to be part of the universal human condition.

Hawai'i has produced its share of romantic tales. One of the most famous is the story of Halemano and his beloved Kamalālāwalu. Similar to other Hawaiian romances, it is a long one, with numerous descriptions of places in the Hawaiian Islands. The descriptions may refer to the emotions and thoughts of the speaker, as well as to Hawaiian geography, giving a poetic cast to the bones of the plot. Here is a summary of the story about Halemano and Kamalālāwalu:

On the island of Hawai'i, in the district of Puna, a daughter was born to two members of royalty and she was given the name of Kamalālāwalu. As was common with women of high rank, a kapu was put upon her when she reached a certain age, so that she would remain a virgin until a suitable marriage could be arranged. No one was allowed to approach her, except for her little brother and eight hundred dogs that were set about to guard her.

She was so beautiful that the chiefs of Hilo and Puna sent presents to her and her family, each hoping to make her his wife. Evidently they were both encouraged to continue waiting for her. Kamalālāwalu amused herself in her isolation with the chiefly sport of surfing. No doubt she also amused herself with daydreams about the hero who one day would claim her as his bride.

On the island of O'ahu, there was an extremely handsome young man named Halemano. He, too, had dreams, although his came at night. In them, the beautiful Kamalālāwalu had appeared repeatedly, and he had fallen in love with her. As time went by, he grew increasingly infatuated with the woman of his dreams. Gradually his dreams became more alive than his waking life and he wanted only to sleep, to be with his beloved. Even when awake, he thought of her constantly and rejected all food, forgetting to feed his body. Without food, he soon wasted away and died.

Fortunately, Halemano's sister, Laenini, was a sorceress. When she learned of her brother's death, she applied her abilities in healing magic and brought him back to life. He told her about the woman of his dreams and she asked him questions about his mysterious love. Halemano described what the woman was wearing, and from this, Laenini was able to trace Kamalālāwalu to her home on the island of Hawai'i.

The sister turned herself into a fish and by magic and cunning was able to enter Kamalālāwalu's house. Then she returned to her human form and spoke to the lovely woman. In so doing, Laenini determined that Kamalālāwalu was indeed the woman of her brother's dreams.

When she returned to Halemano, Laenini advised him how to capture his dream love. After extensive planning and various tricks, Halemano abducted Kamalālāwalu and took her to O'ahu. There their marriage was celebrated with gifts and rejoicing, for the two young people were now lovers.

The ruling chief of O'ahu heard about Kamalālāwalu's great beauty and sent for her, but she refused to obey him, choosing instead to stay with Halemano. The insulted chief sent his army to kill them, and the lovers were forced to flee. They traveled from one island to another, never settling down long enough to reap of

the harvest of crops they had planted. Finally they traveled back to the island of Hawai'i.

But love was anything but true. Kamalālāwalu was enticed away from Halemano several times, going from a lover, back to her husband, and then later to another lover. This last lover was the chief of Puna, but she did not stay long with him either. In the manner of the early Hawaiians, each time Kamalālāwalu went to another lover she became his wife.

With the last betrayal, the grieved Halemano again refused to eat. As he yearned for his absent wife, he sickened and was soon dead. Again his sorceress sister brought him back to life. She proposed that he learn the hula and become a master of hula chants and songs in order to win back his wife's love. Halemano followed his sister's advice and studied diligently. After the *'ūniki* (graduation exercises), he became a famous singer and chanter.

As time passed, Halemano began to court the daughter of a high chief and she became enamored of him. At a game of *kilu*, where men and women played against each other for a predetermined prize, often that of sexual encounter, Halemano and the chief's daughter were the contestants. They had already decided that whoever won the game would win possession of the other as a mate. The entire island had been invited to participate and to witness the prize-taking of Halemano and the chief's daughter.

Kamalālāwalu was among those who went to the kilu game. She heard Halemano chant, longed for him again, and wanted to return to him.

> Alas, O my love!
> My love of the home where we were friendless,
> Our only friend being our love for one another.
> It is hooked and it bites to the very inside of the bones.
> O my love, speak to me!

When Halemano saw Kamalālāwalu again, he was struck anew by her beauty, which far eclipsed that of the new woman in his life. As he played at kilu against the chief's daughter, his chants were not directed toward her. Rather, he chanted numerous love songs in which he described his love for his former wife and the life they had spent together.

> Love is like a chief, it is prized highly,
> For it is the screen by night and by day.
> O my love, come back,
> For love is like food that cannot be taken!

Kamalālāwalu was deeply moved, and weeping she indicated that she wanted to return to him. Halemano, however, was already claimed by the daughter of the chief, and Kamalālāwalu was forced to leave.

Sometime later, Halemano managed to escape from his fiercely possessive new wife and he fled to another island. Kamalālāwalu also left the island of Hawai'i, perhaps searching for him. After traveling to various islands and continuously missing one another, they finally met again on the island of Kaua'i. They spoke in a friendly manner, but Halemano refused to take Kamalālāwalu back as his wife. By now it was he who was weary of her.

Saddened, she returned to O'ahu, where she became the wife of yet another chief. When the chiefs of Puna and Hilo learned of her whereabouts, they went to O'ahu with a mighty army and slaughtered many people on O'ahu. The two chiefs, who had been Kamalālāwalu's original suitors, found her alive and took her with them back to the island of Hawai'i (adapted from Elbert 1959).

The story certainly does not end with the familiar note of Western tales, "and so they lived happily ever after." Very few Hawaiian romances are resolved in such a tidy manner. Similar to the way our ears are trained to expect certain musical patterns, they are also trained to anticipate certain literary patterns. In an analogy to music, the romance of Halemano does not end with a tonal chord. Inasmuch as few, if any, lovers really do live happily ever after in actual life, whether in early Hawai'i or modern New York, the yearning for eternal happiness may say something about the psychology of human beings who so imagine it.

Although the legend of Halemano seems to be told in a minor key, it has a familiar ring to it, as though it were a story about one of our neighbors or relatives, or even about ourselves. Remember cousin George who fell in love with the beautiful Elizabeth and called her his little princess? And then remember how Elizabeth became bored with George and, wanting more excitement in her life, embarked upon a series of love affairs that poked holes in their rowboat of matrimony? When the boat finally sank, everyone got wet and maybe one of the characters in the drama drowned.

In the Hawaiian tale, Halemano dreamed of his love and then managed to find a woman who precisely matched the one in his dreams. At first he seemed to have extraordinary luck, not only did he find her, but he claimed her as his bride. Despite the passion that developed between them, however, their perfect romance fell apart quickly. To one degree or another, a similar story takes place when any of us finally finds Mr. or Ms. Absolutely Right. We may stay together, having committed ourselves for "better or for worse," but the breathlessly perfect quality of the relationship usually changes in unforeseen ways. The perfect fit we may have felt when we first fell in love begins to shake loose like a jigsaw puzzle picture. The pieces gradually tumble out of the picture that we have formed in our minds.

Herein lies the problem: the picture is formed in our minds and is not a true representation of the actual situation. There are three Jungian concepts that can explain what happened to Halemano, cousin George, or any of us when involved in affairs of the heart. They are the psychological dynamics of the *anima*, the *animus*, and *projection*.

Traditional Hawaiian thought is based upon the knowledge of the duality of all life. The duality of the masculine and feminine principles is expressed in numerous ways, although it probably does not extend to a recognition of such duality within each person. Now, however, we can understand that all of us are androgynous in the sense that we each combine both masculine and feminine elements. We know this is true biologically and it is also true psychologically. The contrasexual elements—in a man his feminine characteristics, and in a woman her masculine characteristics—are more or less recessive. A man's inner woman, his own feminine side, is called the *anima*. The inner man in a woman, which is her own masculine side, is called the *animus*.

The words *anima* and *animus* imply qualities of soul, spirit, life, and breath. These are qualities that bring aliveness and meaningfulness to what would otherwise be a mundane existence. It seems almost impossible to define what is meant by "masculine" or "feminine," because each culture attaches different meanings to these terms. All cultures, however, agree that there is a difference between the two principles and that the adjective *masculine* most often is associated with men and maleness, while the adjective *feminine* is most often associated with women and femaleness. For the moment, this may be as clear a distinction as we can collectively agree upon.

Because the anima and animus are archetypal images, which are hidden inside the dark recesses of our inner homes, we can only experience them indirectly. We find them in our dreams or fantasies, where they often appear as figures of the opposite sex; and when we know what to look for, we can find them in our behavior and in the behavior of others. Relevant to an understanding of the plight of Halemano and Kamalālāwalu, we also find such inner partners projected upon other people.

As understood in terms of Jungian psychology, we do not *make* projections in the sense of throwing something out into the world. Rather, we meet unknown parts of ourselves in another person or situation, and it is there that we get our first chance to see them. Such projected content has an unusually strong positive or negative impact upon us.

Halemano encountered Kamalālāwalu in the outer world, as well as in his dreams, so he was dealt a double blow which would have overpowered any mortal man. The drama in his dreams gave him his first experience of Kamalālāwalu as a reflection of his own anima/soul. The outer woman reinforced the impact upon him because she, too, represented a reflection of something hidden in himself. Kamalālāwalu, as a separate, individual woman, not as a reflection of his anima, remained a stranger.

As is the case with most men, Halemano had no knowledge of his own feminine elements and only found them reflected in dreams or in actual women. Elements that we do not recognize in ourselves project themselves whenever they encounter a suitable hook, meaning a certain correspondence between the inner and outer realities. Then, as is said in the chant, we are hooked, sharply bitten to the very inside of our bones.

When a man falls in love with a woman, his anima/soul is hooked by its resemblance to the woman and, in effect, he falls in love with his own soul. The actual woman is hidden behind a reflecting mirror. What he perceives is not the flesh-and-blood human being, but all of the unrecognized aspects of his own feminine nature. Moreover, since many such projections are collective, meaning that they reflect how all women are supposed to be in a particular society, the projection is further distorted and the woman's individual personality remains shadowed. Being an archetypal image, the anima consists of both positive and negative aspects, and when the real woman shows her own personality, the man perceives an increasing number of negative qualities about her. As before, these may be projections from within himself.

It is no wonder that Halemano had problems with his women.

Halemano found his soul reflected in the face and form of Kamalālāwalu. She, however, was a human woman, obviously an immature one, and his faulty vision led to considerable suffering.

A similar process takes place in women, who are just as likely to find their own hidden masculine side reflected in men. Kamalālāwalu, too, was completely unaware of various aspects of herself, which we would now term the animus. Isolated and waiting to be claimed by one of two chiefs, she must have fantasized about the royal suitor who would finally come for her and take her as his bride. While she frolicked in the ocean and played with her little brother and eight hundred dogs, she probably imagined a life of romance and excitement with her as-yet-unseen lover.

When Halemano first abducted her, the glamour of the new experience must have encouraged an immediate projection upon the handsome stranger, especially since she had been isolated from men for a long time. Undoubtedly it seemed like falling in love, and apparently she remained in an enchanted state during the honeymoon period on Oʻahu. The story informs us that she resisted the command of the Oʻahu chief, which was a sacred duty to obey in old Hawaiʻi, and refused to appear before him. If she had done so, it is obvious that she would have been taken away from her new husband. Evidently the romance began to fall apart for Kamalālāwalu when she and her young husband were forced to flee into exile, loneliness, hardship, and poverty. Certainly there was nothing in her background to prepare her for such a life.

Thereafter, Kamalālāwalu seized every opportunity to become the wife of a chief, thus living out what were probably her earlier fantasies. There is something compulsive about Kamalālāwalu's serial relationships, as if a happily-ever-after theme played itself repeatedly within her, causing her to search again and again for the expected bliss. When Halemano deviated from her invisible script, Kamalālāwalu abandoned him and continued to act out her own predetermined role.

At the point in the story when they met again on Kauaʻi and calmly discussed what had happened, they finally had an opportunity to create a true marriage, one based upon reality and not on projection. But as is often the case in real life, at this point they separated from each other forever.

Evidently Halemano was unwilling to re-enter a marriage with the woman he had desired for so many years. By now, he must have perceived her faults and inadequacies. The effort needed to create an actual relationship with her might have seemed boring or tedious to him after the hot excitement of grand passion. Kamalālāwalu, however, seems to have fallen in love again, this time with her former husband. Halemano had changed and, as a famous singer and chanter, had become more appealing to her. It is also likely that she found him more attractive because another woman, the chief's daughter, desired him. It is human nature to give added value to someone who is highly valued by others. Kamalālāwalu seems to have looked upon Halemano with new eyes as soon as he was not easily available for her whims and mood swings.

In the same way that Kamalālāwalu and Halemano had missed each other when they traveled from island to island, they also missed each other in their emotional connections. And as they had never settled down long enough to harvest the crops they had planted during their marriage, so later they did not stay together and reap the rewards they might have given one another as limited human beings in a real human engagement. In such a manner does art reflect life.

We stir up similar problems for ourselves continuously. We fall in love blindly, we fall into boredom or despair compulsively, we miss each other's essential humanness because we belittle it, and then we separate without reaping the harvest of knowledge. At best, too many of us stay together out of fear or inertia, while continuing to fantasize about romantic bliss.

We may yearn endlessly for the "significant other" who will bring fulfillment, and we may never become aware of the inner partner who might fulfill that yearning. Such an inner mate has elements of the divine and therefore can be a carrier of ecstasy. The anima and animus are archetypal images, coming as they do from the deepest levels of the psyche, and no mere mortal will ever rival the numinous aura of a god or goddess.

Hawaiians personified the inner partners, which, being archetypal, are found universally. They believed in spirit lovers, the *kāne o ka pō* (husband of the night) and the *wahine o ka pō* (wife of the night). These spirit lovers might come to a woman or man during the night and claim a human being as a mate. The human woman or man developed a relationship with that spirit lover, one that included sexual intercourse as well as loving communication. Sometimes, as was the case with Halemano, the human mate fell so desperately in love with the spirit lover that he or she lost appetite for food, as well as for life. Unless others took immediate action, the person sickened and soon died. Various methods of exorcism were used to combat what was, essentially, possession by an autonomous spirit. There are a number of interesting accounts of Hawaiian men and women who had marital relationships with spirit lovers and then suffered strange consequences as a result.

Evidently the union between spirit lover and human woman sometimes produced a child. These were special children, who either were returned to the spirit world from which the lover had come (from a certain viewpoint, this would appear like sending the child to death) or were raised as "different" with special destinies. Any comments I might make about such biological miracles would sound cynical, although I have witnessed the profound power of psychological spirit lovers over the destinies of modern women.

The Hawaiians understood that the spirit lovers might have a positive, as well as a negative, effect upon the dreamer. Although most often the relationship between spirit lover and human being appears to have been a sexual one, frequently it was also one of communication and guidance. Then the spirit lover held long conversations with the dreaming mate, offering help and advice about the dreamer's daily life (Handy and Pukui 1972; Pukui, Haertig, and Lee 1972).

On a less dramatic level, we can witness similar dynamics in our own dreams. At a time of drastic changes in her life, a woman dreamed:

> I'm with familiar people and we're celebrating something. A tall, dark man appears who is very attractive. He had been my lover previously and I feel a sort of desperate love for him. How does he feel about me? We dance and hold each other closely as we waltz in grand, free movements to music that comes from an invisible orchestra. I feel a strong physical attraction for this man and wonder if we'll make love tonight. I'm aware that we're being watched by another man who is indistinct and evidently new to my life. There is a sense of steadfastness and dependability to the second man.
>
> After the first man and I stop dancing, something is said which informs me that the dark man will never marry me, or otherwise commit himself to me, and that I must separate myself from him.

Somehow I do pull apart from him and then I cry and cry, mourning him as my lost love.

There are ramifications to this dream that are unique to the circumstances of the dreamer, but basically it expresses the strong emotion that can bind a living woman to the spirit lover who dwells within her own unconscious psyche. The dark man with whom she dances has acted as a vampire, holding her in captive fascination while draining vitality from her life. The lure of his charming promises, the excitement of the dance they share, and the seduction of his godlike spirit have had negative effects upon her. She has been unable to form a committed relationship with any human man, because the glamour of her spirit lover has prevented her from appreciating the common flesh of her own kind. No mortal man could possibly compete with the godlike image operating within the woman's expectations.

Even worse, she has lived a provisional life, never fully committing herself to the fulfillment of any goal that requires ongoing, nitty-gritty work and dedication. In her dream, the appearance of the second man holds the promise of a more steadfast attitude, which she might find within herself and for herself in the future. But first she must mourn her lost love, because a dark relationship with a spirit lover has its moments of bliss, and to be exiled from paradise brings a sense of loss, grief, and even disorientation.

The second man in the woman's dream might have been more spirit guide than spirit lover. As the Hawaiians understood, the husband or wife of the night could be a positive force in a human life. It is up to us and our attitude toward these inner spirits whether they help or hinder us in our human concerns. As is the case with relationships in outer reality, we need to separate ourselves from symbiotic entanglements before true relating can occur. A symbiotic union is shadowy; it takes place in the night, and there is no space between the "I" and the "Other" for air to flow or growth to occur. Dark forces such as these are negative, even though they feel comfortable, because whatever is going on is invisible. When the light, created by separation, begins to illuminate what belongs to the spirit world and what belongs to the human world, then we are able to make more conscious choices about our lives and have more determination over our fates.

A man, who was beginning to separate himself from a lifelong enslavement to his own cloudy and moody feminine aspects, had the following dream:

> Somehow I had gotten on the wrong path and now I'm lost in a dense jungle. Nighttime is approaching and soon it will be completely dark and I still can't find my way out. I hear the sounds of animals and know that they're dangerous. Maybe I see a snake. I stop and look around. My fear is mounting steadily and I can hear my heart pounding in my ears. Suddenly a light comes toward me out of the jungle, and gradually I can see that a lovely, young woman, dressed in a flowing white robe, is holding a round flashlight. She takes my hand and says that she'll guide me to safety.

When a man, such as the dreamer, is able to relate to what the lovely woman represents within himself, she can guide him in his relationships with other people, as well as with whatever comes his way in life. If the reflection from his anima is not cast completely upon the women he encounters, he will be able to perceive women more clearly and conduct himself more consciously. In effect, he will seem more manly, or in better relationship with his own manhood. The dream indicates that such a new development is a possibility, although he has not yet found his path or his way out of the jungle.

The woman in the man's dream has goddesslike qualities, and the handsome dancer in the woman's dream resembles a spirit lover. We become fascinated when we perceive such qualities in another person. If, however, the spirit or deity remains projected upon another human being, there is hell as well as heaven to pay. All such projections are a heavy burden, which most men and women cannot carry comfortably for long.

Initially we may behave as though we were indeed the deity projected upon us. It is tempting to do so because such a projection gives us a tremendous amount of power. It amounts to having ultimate power over another person's destiny. If I am seen as a goddess, then I can rule another's life and he is my captive. Although the atmosphere is a bit thin up on a pedestal, it brings a headiness which can make the least of us feel like the grandest. But we are not gods and goddesses, and the higher we mount, the harder we tumble when the negative aspects of the archetypal image begin to surface.

When the recipient of such a projection refuses to carry the godlike reflection any longer, or if the true human personality splits the seams of the confining role, then the love affair usually ends or the marriage is in for rough times. As the projections fall away, we discover that an all-too-human being is sharing bed, board, and the daily problems of human, not heavenly, existence. If we can no longer find the gods and goddesses in heaven or in other human beings, we are forced to discover them somewhere in ourselves, and it is at this point that everything changes.

Now we can begin to make appropriate choices and decide how to utilize the energy contained in the spirit lovers. It is our human perspective that decides whether the anima and animus are to be positive or negative when we live with them in the daylight. As the projections drop away, we can discover that an actual relationship with a human partner gives us the most fertile possible ground within which to discover the hidden parts of ourselves. When we find out what has been projected upon another person, we can begin to discover who we really are.

In the story about Halemano, his sister acted as a helpful guide for him. She healed him, she led him to his lady love, and then she encouraged him to become a noted chanter and singer. Such helpful females are found frequently in Hawaiian tales, wherein a sister, mother, grandmother, or even wife gives the hero the guidance he needs to complete his heroic task. As a result of his sister's assistance, Halemano changed in regard to his work and creative fulfillment. His relationship with women, however, seems as undeveloped as it had been at the beginning of the story.

The fate of Kamalālāwalu is even more illustrative of what happens when the challenge to change is ignored. She ended up where she began, on the island of Hawai'i, and a captive of the original two suitors. We can assume that she was older, but not much wiser, and that if possible, she would continue her previous pattern. Her parents and the two suitors seem to have controlled her fate from beginning to end.

The melody continues to sound familiar. The story of Halemano and Kamalālāwalu is painfully true to life. Perhaps the crucial issue lies in the word *change*. Halemano changed by becoming a more creative man, and on that level his life became more vital. Kamalālāwalu was unable to change in any way. As a result, her existence became a repetitious series of identical responses, which seem monotonous and increasingly like a living death. From the perspective of the one who moves, the very steps leading to change can seem like death, but of another kind, one that leaves the familiar ground behind and steps into unknown territory. This idea is expressed in the myth by Hale-mano's two deaths and two rebirths.

There is another myth that expresses more about lovers and death, symbolic or otherwise. Myths in which a hero descends to the underworld in an attempt to bring back the soul of a beloved woman are found throughout the world. Hawai'i is no exception. One such myth is the story of Hiku and Kāwelu. It has a plot similar to numerous other Polynesian stories, so we can assume that they all spring from a common mythologem buried in the Polynesian past.

> Hiku of the forest had a charmed arrow which led him down the mountain to the seashore, straight to the home of Kāwelu, a lovely young chiefess. They fell in love and lived together for a while. Hiku soon left her, however, either because he missed his mountain home or because she refused to have sexual intercourse with him. Kāwelu tried to follow him up the mountain, but he caused heavy vines and vegetation to grow, entrapping her until he disappeared from her sight. Grief-stricken, Kāwelu returned home and hanged herself with a piece of vine.
>
> When Hiku learned of her death, he was filled with remorse and set off for the underworld to recover her soul. First he covered himself with the oil of a rancid coconut so that he would smell like a dead man and not arouse the suspicions of the inhabitants of the underworld. Then he gave one end of a long vine to his friends and lowered the other end into the underworld. Using the vine as a swing, he tricked Kāwelu's spirit into joining him on it. They swung higher and higher as he gave a signal to his friends, who pulled Kāwelu and him up to the land of the living. To prevent Kāwelu's soul from escaping, he trapped it inside a split coconut shell.
>
> Hiku hurried to the home of his beloved and forced her soul back into her dead body. He did this in the accustomed manner, forcing her soul into the great toe of her left foot, and then massaging it up into her body until it reached her heart. Gradually Kāwelu came back to life and the two were reunited. They lived together contentedly for the rest of their lives (adapted from Beckwith 1970; Handy 1985; Westervelt 1963a).

The myth can be understood on several levels. On the surface, it is a universal love story. In contrast to the myth about Orpheus and Eurydice, and hundreds of similar tales told throughout history, the Hawaiian story has a happy ending. As a romance, it tells about a repentant hero who braves the perils of the underworld in order to bring his sweetheart back to life.

On a deeper level, it is apparent that there are overtones of shamanistic behavior in Hiku's adventures. Vertical flight, either of ascending to the upperworld or of descending to the underworld, are found universally among shamans. Such vertical flights are an essential element in shamanistic healing. Often the shaman's purpose is to enter into the spirit world at great risk to him- or herself in order to catch a departed soul, which is then forced back into the dead body. Hiku's power as a shaman is obvious in his ability to undertake such a perilous task and to successfully revive Kāwelu in the manner often used by shamanistic healers.

A shaman's initial journey frequently involves such vertical travel as a means to heal himself. It is understood that in order to heal others, a shaman's own wounds must first be healed. To extend the meaning further, psychologically we can understand Hiku's adventure as a descent into the underworld of his own dark psyche. At this point, if we consider the myth from a psychological view, Hiku's soul becomes identical in meaning with Kāwelu's soul (in the story), and his journey becomes one of finding his anima/soul within the darkness of the unconscious psyche.

In some versions of the myth, Hiku and Kāwelu are brother and sister. Although they had not met previously, they were destined for each other because they were both of very high rank. In old Hawai'i, when close relatives were members of the highest royalty, a marriage between them was the only way in which the powerful mana could be reinforced and not diluted by a mate of lesser rank. The mana had come to them from the gods, and they were the carriers of that mana within each generation. When a man and a woman who possessed mana in equal amount produced children, the chiefly power would be passed on to their offspring intact, or even increased. As royal brother and sister, Hiku and Kāwelu may be seen as two parts of the same archetypal image, the masculine and feminine elements of divine royalty. That image, like any symbol, is elusive of precise definition, but it is a powerful expression of royal wholeness.

From the standpoint of the feminine (Kāwelu), she attempted to hold on to her human lover, but was unable to do so. In her anguish at losing him, she committed suicide, which on a symbolic level implies a need to kill off a previous way of living her life. Unable to reach her heart's desire, she became depressed, meaning she was flung into the depths of her own psyche. Under similar circumstances, we are all vulnerable to such a descent, which feels like dropping into hell. It seems like a mortal wound, causing considerable anguish and suffering. When we are in such a depressed state, we seem to be among the nonliving, and we wonder if we will ever again feel sunlight on our face. When in the throes of such depression, all hope and joy are left far above on an almost forgotten level of existence, and we question whether the depression will ever end. In Kāwelu's case, she was saved by an aspect of herself, her own masculine qualities, the animus, here personified by Hiku.

As an example of how an equivalent scenario would read in human terms, a woman may be deeply disappointed in a love affair. The desired man has abandoned her for one or more of many possible reasons and she may be bewildered by his actions. It is more than possible that something in her own personality contributed to the sad outcome of the romance. Either she was too dependent or too demanding, or perhaps too superficial. Or she may be one of the women who always seems to choose a man who is incapable of a lasting commitment. Whatever the reason, the loss of that particular man has opened a trapdoor in her psychological house and she has plummeted into depression. Unless she is foolish enough to act out the suicidal impulse, her stay in the underworld may ultimately lead to a new way to live her life. Her own previously undeveloped qualities may save her and bring her to psychological rebirth. With a different perspective and an enlarged personality, she will become more autonomous. She may find new value in her own work and goals, and it is likely that she will be ready to commit herself to a more realistic relationship with an appropriate man.

With equal validity, we can view the myth of Hiku and Kāwelu from the masculine perspective. Hiku behaved in a grossly immature manner. Either he wanted to go back to his childhood home on the mountain, where his mother lived, or he sulked peevishly because Kāwelu refused his sexual advances. In either case, his behavior was totally egocentric. Although he may have "fallen in love" with the lovely young woman, he certainly did not love her. In addition, his behavior would indicate that he had no relationship with his own soul, and, as a result, he was unable to see the reality of the actual woman he thought he desired.

In this case, Hiku's descent into the underworld would represent a journey into his own depths, into a place where he was no longer able to live his life in the same way. His relationship to the place of death is indicated by the rancid oil that he rubbed on his skin, signifying that he had taken on the semblance of a dead person. The vine swing, whereby he lowered himself and then brought the soul of his beloved up to the world of the living, is a perfect image of the axis that connects the underworld, human world, and upperworld in all shamanistic and magical experiences. By taking possession of his own soul, Hiku healed himself. He would not have been restored to his former condition; rather, he would have become a different person thereafter.

At a deep level, there is no conflict between the feminine or masculine perspectives when dealing with such a myth. There is a dynamic which is the same in all of us, whether we are women or men. The mythological verity is a human truth, which operates within us and for us. Until something forces us to descend into ourselves and grasp some portion of our missing parts, we are incomplete, always needing to find those qualities in another person.

Such a journey is ongoing, because we will never be able to take complete possession of whatever the anima and animus represent. We will always find our own hidden aspects projected onto another person, and therein lies the excitement and potential of human relationships. They can evolve as we struggle and grow with a chosen mate.

We can change the way we sing our own songs. It is true that falling in love is a happening, but it is also true that learning to love may be the most rewarding lesson we can learn in this lifetime.

> There was a seeking of the lost, now it is found—
> A mate is found,
> One to share the chills of winter . . .
> Love has made a plea that you two become united.
> Here is a perch, a heavenly resting place,
> A perch, a perch in heaven . . .
> There are sounds of voices in an inhabited house,

But what voices are heard in any empty one?
You two are now one,
The darkness has begun to depart,
The east is beginning to brighten
For day is here at last! . . .
You are wedded! . . .
The prayer has gone its way.

                    From an ancient marriage chant
                    (Handy and Pukui 1972)

5

Māui,
Light-bringer
of the Pacific

A Hawaiian legend tells us that when people were first created they were able to stand upright, but they were unable to move. Their legs and arms had no joints and were bound tightly to their bodies by weblike skin. The demigod Māui was disgusted with them and attacked the immobile creatures. He broke legs, arms, elbows, knees, and hips, loosening up bodies and creating joints. The webs were destroyed. At last the people could move around from place to place and take care of their needs. No longer were they as motionless as stiff trees, standing in a row (adapted from Luomala 1971).

WHO was this passionate demigod who dared to tear human beings away from their original static web? There are thousands of stories told in the Pacific region about Māui, the demigod hero of the islands. Polynesian mythology is rich and dramatic; a pantheon of colorful deities inhabit the land, waters, and skies of the Pacific, but Māui is the most varied and famous.

I first encountered Māui on the Hawaiian island that bears his name. It was near the scene of one of his great adventures, on the slopes of the enormous dormant volcano, Haleakalā (House of the sun). That was quite a few years ago, before I moved to Hawai'i, and increasingly I have been drawn to a mysterious essence within the mythologem that bears the name of Māui.

I suspect that some of my involvement with Māui is connected with another image that has been moving in my mind for about as many years as I have known the demigod. In this image, people (fellow residents of my culture, and sometimes I am there too) are trying to balance on the top of a large and slippery plastic bubble. The bubble rises high above the ground and although there is something beneath the people's feet, it is not very solid and provides little support. As a result, the people continuously slide around and are easy prey for any pseudomessiah or simple system that comes along and promises security. The life of the past, of our human heritage which would offer real support, remains below the bubble, buried within our common ground.

It was while I was finding my own way off the bubble that Māui came into my life. Or perhaps it would be more accurate to say that I chanced into the part of life where Māui still exists—and rages at people caught by webs.

The Māui myths originated in an early and important time in human experience, when a divine child was born who came to redeem and transform, bringing with him a different life vision and a new conscious point of view. Those of us who were raised within Judeo-Christian mythology sometimes have difficulty experiencing our traditional symbols as still alive and relevant. Even classical mythology often speaks to us in signs instead of symbols because we have traveled its roads so frequently. "Zeus is the husband of Hera," we repeat. "Take two steps to the left and find Athene being born out of Zeus' head."

Māui takes us further back, to an unfamiliar place, where life still remains untapped by our benumbed senses. Māui does not live on the slippery surface of a plastic bubble nor even in our well-marked books. He would be furious with the way we often use our arms and legs, to slip and slide and manipulate our bodies, and not go anywhere at all. Māui's origin is rooted in the time before recorded history. As such, within our own psyches, he originates at a deep and primitive level. Nowhere is it written, or even told, where the stories about Māui began. Even the origin of his name is obscure, although the interpretation I like best is that it might refer to "the left hand."

When the Polynesians first began to voyage across the Pacific, long before the beginning of the Christian era, Māui was already an established part of their mythology. And no one is certain where the Polynesians themselves originated. Māui legends began in prehistory and have persisted with remarkable consistency and vitality across a vaster area of the world than have those of any other ancient hero or god. Stories of his exploits are found in all of Polynesia and in various parts of Melanesia and Micronesia, primarily on those islands that have been influenced by Polynesian culture.

Māui defied the more ancient and established gods, the akua,

and in so doing he frequently enriched humankind. It was he who fished up islands from the sea. In addition, he stole the sacred fire, snared the sun, raised the sky from the earth, trapped the winds, changed terrain, founded dynasties, made useful inventions and tools, killed dragonlike monsters, and, in the manner of such spirits, he changed easily into other forms, usually into a bird. Most early Pacific islanders, with local embellishments, claimed that Māui was the demigod who pulled their home island out of the ocean.

In all of Polynesia, and even beyond, there is no hero as famous as he. Māui-tiki-tiki, he is called, or Māui-tinihanga, Māui-of-a-thousand-tricks. He has hundreds of names and epithets, and more tricks by far than names. In Hawai'i he is often known as Māui-a-ka-malo (Māui-of-the-loincloth).

Indeed he is a trickster! He has brought me stories about himself from various places in Polynesia, not only from Hawai'i. Insisting that these various myths are related to each other because he is a pan-Pacific hero, he has influenced me to include elements of these stories in what I have recorded about him. Similar to other tricksters, he is not to be denied lest our lives become predictable and drab. What follows, then, are stories from Hawai'i, often overlapping with each other, and several from other places in the vast region that the demigod has claimed as his own, while he was changing the lives of his people.

Māui's mother conceived him, her last son, in a strange manner. It is said that one day she went down to the sea to gather seaweed. There she found a red *malo*, the tapa loincloth worn by men. Red is a sacred color, associated with the gods and chiefs, so a strong force must have led her to wrap the malo around her own waist. Then she lay down to sleep. "All alone," she told her husband, and who could doubt such an innocent story?

The child so conceived was born long before full term, and his mother took the pathetic little miscarriage back down to the sea. Then she cut off her hair, and tying it around him, she gave him to the waves. But he did not drown. He was protected by the jellyfish until he was found by his ancestor gods, including the great god of the sea. He was taken to the god's own home and shaped there into human form and taught the secrets of magic. Years passed as Māui grew strong and clever and almost, but not quite, the same as the great gods of that place.

Little Māui was not content to live with the deities indefinitely.

The human part of him cried out for human warmth, so, while still a boy, he went back to his mother's land. There he found his mother and brothers, and he followed them wherever they went, finally following them home, although he was not allowed to enter. Later his brothers played with him. They all made spears from canes and began to throw them at the house as a target. Of course, it was a game and the slender spears fell back from the grass thatch covering the house; they fell to the ground like playthings. Then Māui recited an incantation, and his magic power toughened his spear and made it heavy. He flung it against the house, and, like a flash of lightning tearing at a cloud, his spear penetrated the family home, creating a large hole.

His mother came outside to drive the strange boy away. Polynesians describe Māui as a small, precocious, ugly, flat-headed boy who had, however, the bold and flashing eyes of a warrior. In the manner of such a warrior, he now drew himself straight and announced himself as her son. His mother saw him for what he was, her own child who had the great mana of his ancestors, they who were gods. She laid her hands upon him, and pressing her nose against his nose, she claimed him as her own (adapted from Colum 1973; Luomala 1971:30–31).

In the *Kumulipo*, we hear of Māui's birth in a different way.

Here, his mother, Hina-i-ke-ahi (Hina-in-the-fire) was herself of divine descent. She and her husband had four children, all boys. The youngest, Māui-a-ka-malo, was born as an egg that hatched into a bird and next assumed human form. Hina was surprised, she had not even known that she was pregnant. Perhaps she had forgotten the loincloth that she had found on the beach. Inasmuch as Hina was related to the *'alae* (mudhens), the birdlike quality of her child should not have surprised her. When she showed the loincloth to her husband, he called it a gift from the gods, a sign that their child would have great mana (adapted from Luomala 1971).

The stories about Māui have a characteristic flavor, so despite numerous variations upon themes, certain motifs appear with frequency and may be seen as part of a heroic cycle. No matter what the plot (which varies from island to island), Māui's birth is unusual, as befits the arrival of a special or divine child. In this sense, he has been compared to various other mythological heroes: Jesus, Moses, Mercury, and Hercules. Māui is always depicted as the youngest child in a family of brothers. He is often

portrayed as striving for family acceptance, which is another
familiar motif in myths and fairy tales, because it indicates that
the hero brings a new element that is needed before the next de-
velopmental phase can begin. Invariably the new element is initially rejected, because it is unknown and thus feared.

*Māui is a hero, then, born to throw a spear into the Mother's
house. Conceived within a miracle, within the watery womb,
within the moist mist of the Mother of us all. Born of the waters
of life. Born as egg, a new beginning. Māui-a-ka-malo, born as
new consciousness, bright bearer of light.*

Before long, the new hero began to change the world into
which he was born. It is said that when Māui was young, the sky
was so low that the leaves of the trees were flattened as they
pressed against the sky. Even worse, the land was very dark, and
people had to crawl around in the narrow space between heaven
and earth.

Sometimes it is said that a secret name was tattoed on Māui's
arm and that this name filled him with superhuman physical
power. Whatever the source of his strength, he was powerful
enough to lift the sky. First, he pushed the sky to the tops of
trees, then to where the mountains now have their highest
peaks. Finally, he pushed again with a mighty effort and lifted
the skies to where we see them now, fully separated from the
ground.

Then people were able to walk all over the land and stand tall.
The clouds no longer rested upon the ground and people had clear
air to breathe and light with which to see.

As with the myths about Kāne, Wākea, and numerous other
phallic (in the sense of procreation) sky gods, many of the Māui
stories relate to daytime and sunlight. Throughout Polynesia
these are associated with the masculine principle and with
bright, positive energy. Universally light of day and sun have
symbolized consciousness, being aware and awake, and new real-
ization. By overcoming the dark, unknowing state, Māui over-
came an earlier unconscious condition and brought the light of
awareness. This is a motif that is repeated in so many ways
among various mythologies that the message seems to be an
urgent one: as time passes, the bright light of morning becomes
the dusk of evening, and after the long night, another heroic
light-bringer is needed.

In the fashion of such light-bringers, Māui stood on the very edge of the known world, and he stood there alone. In the evolution of human beings, he seems to personify a particular point in psychological time, a place where man and gods touch and meet, struggle and change. When the demigod lifted the sky, when he separated the original symbiotic unity of the primal parents, in an echo of Tane's (the Maori Kāne) feat, it was a moment of labor and pain, and again of new birth.

Kāne is a god, so, despite his achievement, his efforts seem far removed from our human condition. Māui is half-god, half-human, and a culture hero. His accomplishments imply an almost human possibility. He expresses human consciousness standing in the light of awareness of itself, and doing so by human effort. The *I* of ego consciousness was born in that separation, polarity was created, and the light was set free.

Of all the thousands of tricks performed by the demigod, the most famous is the fishing up of land.

Although Māui had already invented many tools that his brothers copied, such as kites for sailing and barbs on spears for fishing, his brothers called him lazy. Often they were exasperated with the way he tricked them into doing his work for him. One day he decided to try some unusual fishing, perhaps to quiet his brothers forever.

But first he needed a fishhook. Sometimes fishhooks were made of a bone taken from the body of someone who, while still alive, had been noted for great mana. Māui went down into the underworld. There he found his ancestress, she who was dead on one side and alive on the other. He took her jawbone from the side that was dead and fashioned his hook from it. There are those who say that his ancestress did not give him her jawbone willingly, but such details never interfered with Māui's plans.

Then he needed special bait. His mother had sacred birds, the 'alae, who were her close relatives, and Māui stole one of them. With his bait and hook well hidden, and with a line made of the strongest *olonā* vines, Māui joined his brothers as they paddled out to sea for the daily fishing. He urged them to paddle farther and farther, encouraging them with the promise of good fishing just ahead. At last he let down his line, the hook baited with the struggling 'alae. The hook sank to where Old One Tooth (Pimoe, a demigod in *ulua* fish form) held the land fast to the bottom of the sea. When the bird approached, Old One Tooth took it in his mouth and was caught by the magic hook.

As soon as Māui felt the pull on his line, he ordered his brothers to paddle their hardest, for he had caught a great fish. He told them not to look back as they paddled, or the fish would be lost. The bottom of the ocean quaked and huge waves bore down on the boat. Again Māui warned his brothers not to look back.

Despite the warnings, one of the brothers could no longer restrain himself. He screamed as he looked back and saw a string of islands, all of those in Hawai'i, rising and falling, riding swiftly on waves as they were dragged along on Māui's hook.

Snap! The charm was broken and the hook slipped out of Old One Tooth's mouth. The islands danced in all directions as Old One Tooth chased them through the sea. When he finally got them under control again, he anchored the islands where we find them today. But if Māui's brother had not looked back, all of the Hawaiian Islands, and perhaps many others too, would have been joined into one very large island, for such was Māui's fine plan (adapted from Luomala 1971).

Most Pacific islanders have their own version of how Māui fished up land. Family genealogies often begin with Māui as the earliest ancestor because he was the hero who fished up the island home where they live.

The Māui stories frequently have the quality of adolescent battle, reflecting a time when mankind itself was evolving from containment within the unending natural round, which is the womb of the Great Mother. This was a time of symbiotic unknowingness in nature. Māui's drama was played during a time in humankind's history when the human ego was bringing itself up above the waterline of the vast maternal ocean. As discussed before, in this sense, ego consciousness for each of us is an island that is miraculously pulled up from invisible depths.

Māui's position in the lengthy genealogical chants of various island groups reflects this idea. He is often found in a pivotal place between the primal gods, the akua, and his own descendants who were chiefs, the human carriers of the divine seeds. Behind him lay the primal gods and before him waited many islands of people.

Those of us who live on islands are continuously presented with an outer representation of such an inner or historical drama. The land beneath my feet seems particularly precious just because it is not engulfed by the surrounding ocean. I am constantly reminded of the power and danger of that ocean, the lure of the shoreline, and the relative safety of the land. Here in

Hawai'i, as nowhere else, I have a keen appreciation of the heroic effort needed to pull a piece of land from the vast sea, to dredge a bit of ego consciousness from the unending water.

In our lives, such heroism takes a multitude of forms. It is found at the crucial intersection when a person takes absolute responsibility for his or her own decisions and actions, accepting whatever consequences follow as a result of that step. It may be a statement as deceptively simple as "No." Sometimes it is necessary to say "No" to parents, friends, children, or spouse in order to say "Yes" to one's inner voice. Whenever we automatically act in accord with a prescribed role, whether as mother, father, child, or lover, then we are not aware of the possible choices we can make in individual situations.

The demands of life change constantly, requiring a continual gaze forward. Despite the warnings, Māui's brother looked back, and his curiosity snapped the line. There are times when looking back is regressive, halting the forward movement toward a desired goal. Such behavior is one of no-choice and it makes us pawns of fate.

Conscious choice, on the other hand, often involves conflict and guilt, because it means taking issue with the internalized parental voices, which demand that we be good children forever. Separating from the need for parental approval is difficult even in adulthood; but whoever said it is easy to pull up an island?

Māui did it. That small, precocious, ugly, young demigod dared to take a stand for his own reality. As a mischievous, disrespectful rebel, he took on the most sacred kapu of human beings and gods. He was one of the early heroes to shout a challenge at the maternal cradle of human history. And miraculously, I find an answering echo somewhere in my own soul.

Here in the Pacific, the ancient order of the universe still has its remnants. I am not unique in being lured, almost hypnotically, to journey to this place. The mythological atmosphere throughout Polynesia is one of paradise, and the paradisiacal tradewinds bring the scent of childhood when all was innocent, protected, and eternal. If we listen, Nature herself is the strongest voice speaking.

The attractions of this place are those of an intuited reconnection with the natural world, but they are also those of a primitive past. They seem to touch me, as well as others, where I am most primitive, where I must struggle daily to hold on to conscious goals and commitments, and where I must constantly labor to know that my human nature is not identical to Mother Nature. No wonder Māui brings a sense of recognition. I, too, must find the masculine hero within my own psyche, while I struggle not to sink into the sands of inertia.

It is possible that this sense of recognition is the reason for Māui's longevity. Māui existed as an archetypal image, a universally human behavior pattern, and he still exists somewhere in each of us. The mystery surrounding his origin is reminiscent of the mysterious development of human consciousness itself. Somehow, by a marvelous and unknown process, human beings were born from Pō and emerged to stand among the gods in Ao, and to know the gods and know themselves. This happened to all of humankind and the process repeats itself each time one of us pulls that bit of island from the grip of Old One Tooth.

Early Polynesians believed that the moon, pale and dead in appearance, moved slowly, while the sun, full of life and strength, moved fast. For this reason, days were very short and nights were much too long. Human beings suffered from the fierce heat of the sun and also from the cold of its absence. Night and day alike were a burden to the people. It took years for plants to ripen, and the fishermen had little time for fishing before it was dark and they had to return to shore. Women's tasks were difficult too, because they made the tapa cloth that clothed the people of the land.

Māui watched his mother make the tapa cloth and pitied her because her task was so difficult. Tapa must be thoroughly dried, but the days were so short that rarely could she finish her work in one day. She worked endlessly, trying to move as fast as the sun, but never succeeding.

Māui determined to challenge the sun and force it to extend the length of the days. His mother told him that he would have to prepare for a tremendous battle, and she gave him strands of well-twisted fiber, although some say it was hair from her own head. She told him to go to his grandmother, who lived on Haleakalā, for further assistance.

Māui went to the island that now bears his name. He climbed up Haleakalā to a large *wiliwili* tree and waited through the night. When a rooster crowed three times, his grandmother appeared, carrying a bunch of bananas to cook for her master, the Sun. Māui snatched the bananas away and because his grandmother was blind, she could not find them. "Where are the bananas for the Sun?" she cried.

She broke off more bananas and Māui stole them also. He continued doing this until the old woman was frantic. "Who are you?" she asked, as her nose caught the scent of a man.

"I am Māui, son of Hina-in-the-fire." He explained how he had come to force the Sun to move more slowly.

Recognizing Māui as a hero, his grandmother gave him a magic stone for a battle axe and more rope. Then Māui hid behind the wiliwili tree until the first leg (ray) of the Sun came over the eastern rim of Haleakalā. He caught the leg with a rope and tied it to the tree. One by one the Sun's legs edged over the rim, and one by one they were caught in Māui's nooses. The struggling Sun tried to slide down into the sea again, but he was imprisoned. Then the Sun focused his burning fire upon Māui and they fought long and fiercely. At last Māui began to strike with his axe, and the Sun was forced to plead for his life.

Finally the two contestants entered into an agreement. There would be longer days for part of each year, but for the other part, the wintertime, the Sun could again move quickly. After the morning of that battle, the people had time for everything: the tasks of daylight, such as the drying of tapa cloth, and the lovemaking and sleep of night.

Here again Māui is associated with the sun, with light, and the focused eye of daytime clarity. As expressed in Māui's battle with the sun, clarity of thought and focus of action are won only by a heroic struggle. These are human achievements that can bring joy and meaning to our lives. To call Māui a solar god, as some writers have theorized, is to beg the issue. The Polynesians know that he is only half-god and that he can be described only by recitation of his adventures, many of which are all too human.

He was not worshipped as a deity. In earlier days, he belonged to the people, not to the priests, and people talked about him daily. There were numerous games and songs, as well as puppet shows and contests with complicated string figures, which involved Māui and his many adventures. His trickster qualities delighted his human admirers, for his escapades included sly jokes and malicious pranks. The Maori say that he even changed his brother-in-law into the first dog. Perhaps by a constant recitation of his adventures, people were better able to fight off the moonlight inertia within themselves.

We hear many stories about heroes of other lands who stole fire from the gods and gave that great gift to human beings. And yet Māui gave the fire gift to more people, scattered over more territory, than any other hero. The tales of fire-finding through-out Polynesia are directly connected with Māui under one of his many names, or with one of his important ancestors.

Hawaiians speak of the time when the island people did not know of fire. True, the volcanoes flowed with hot lava, but this story does not mention that. In those days, the people still ate their food raw and often suffered with cold. Sometimes fire was discov-ered accidently, but people did not know how to start it. Only the 'alae, the sacred mudhens of Hina-in-the-fire, knew the secret.

When Māui and his brothers went fishing in those ancient days, they often saw smoke rising from the mountainside. They would rush back to shore, hoping to cook their fish, but all they ever found were the mudhens scratching clay over burned sticks. This happened repeatedly. Each time, the 'alae moved from place to place, making fire only to extinguish it before Māui and his broth-ers reached them. Even when Māui sent his brothers to fish with-out him, he could never catch the birds while they were making their fires. At last he understood that the 'alae counted the men in the canoe and if Māui was missing, they did not cook that day.

The demigod rolled a piece of tapa into the shape of a man and put the cloth on the canoe. Then he hid while his brothers went fishing. In this manner, Māui caught the mudhens before they extinguished their fire. He grabbed one old bird by the neck and threatened to kill her unless she showed him how to make fire. At first the cunning 'alae tried to deceive him. She told him to rub reeds together, then she told him to rub taro leaves together, and then to rub banana stumps together. Naturally, no fire came from such methods, and each time he failed, Māui tightened his hold on the bird's neck.

The battle of wits continued for some time, but at last the 'alae showed Māui which trees contain the fire sticks: the *hau* tree and the sandalwood. Māui used wood from those trees to make his own fire sticks and later taught the Hawaiians how to rub the sticks and start fire. Never again did the people have to eat fish raw and roots uncooked. Do you know what that rascal did with the first stick he lighted? He rubbed it on the head of the mudhen who had given him the secret, and to this day, the 'alae has a red streak across its head (adapted from Luomala 1971; Beckwith 1970).

Throughout the world, early myths and legends indicate that the original fire of humankind was stolen, usually from the gods or from a previous owner, such as an animal or a bird. Repeatedly the original fire was found within a tree, a specific tree, which needed to be shaped into fire sticks. These sticks were always a pair, which required rubbing.

In Hawai'i, the hard-grained fire stick *'au lima* was held upright in the hand and rubbed back and forth upon the hollowed surface of the other fire stick, the softer *'aunaki*, to produce the spark by friction. Aside from its practical use for starting fires, this action also was a perfectly understood sexual image. The friction may also be seen symbolically as the necessary tension needed for any creative act. The tension between a stable conscious ego and a "charged" unconscious psyche brings emotion and suffering, and it is the dynamic necessity for any creation.

In Polynesia, as in other parts of the world, the fire sticks have expressed symbolic aspects of sexual fire, desire, and procreation. An examination of the often explicitly sexual stories related to Māui and to fire making emphasize the sexual and phallic nature of the demigod. In this, he resembles the Greek god Hermes, who is also connected with fire and phallic energy. As is the case with Hermes, the fire of Māui also symbolizes the firing of the spirit and the winged, birdlike aspects of sacred fire.

In our personal lives, the fire spirit manifests in various forms. Many years ago, I was stuck in an accustomed and habitual pattern of behavior. Each day was similar to the preceding one, and my attitude about my life was equally constricted. Although I knew something new was needed, I was afraid to take a step in any direction.

One night I dreamed that I woke up to the sound of giant wings flapping against my bedroom window. My own heart was beating louder than the wings. I knew that a huge angel was out there; it was as though I could see him with absolute clarity. The angel was covered with white feathers, like a bird, but he had the body of a man. This was one of the more frightening experiences of my life, and yet later I was able to open the window of my psychological house and let the new spirit enter.

Although Māui is most often depicted as a child or adolescent, his position as an ancestor is equally important. This is another aspect of the demigod as a creative, masculine spirit. His phallic nature is expressed in numerous stories about his glowing or lopsided penis. Even his trickster qualities are phallic in nature, in that they seem to embody generative power. His most common

Hawaiian name, Māui-a-ka-malo, has the same symbolic impli-
cation. However it is expressed, it is clear that Māui tricked the
gods of their sacred treasure. Generative energy was now available to the people for heat, fertility, and transformation.

*Waiting, hidden, deeply hidden, waiting to be liberated, creat-
ed, re-created into life, into flaming light, waiting to become
awareness, waiting for the creative thrust of Māui-of-the-loincloth.*

Māui's willful nature had led him to innumerable contests
with men and gods. With each success, he became more confi-
dent and defiant, and with each victory, he weakened some of the
power of the ancient gods. From the Maori of New Zealand
comes a story that is found only in fragmented whispers in
Hawai'i, perhaps driven underground with the influx of foreigners.

Māui had heard of the great goddess, she who is called Hina-Nui-
ke-Pō (Great-Hina-of-the-Underworld), and he had been warned
against her. She was said to have the greatest mana, this goddess
who was his own ancestress. Her mana flashed like lightning on
the far horizon, opening and shutting, dangerously blazing against
the distant sky. It was she who brought the death of all creatures
when her mana severed life. But it was also said that if one hero
were to slay her, that hero would live forever and there would be no
more death in all the world.

Māui decided to win everlasting life. Had he not slowed the sun,
lifted the sky, fished up islands, stolen fire, created the dog,
invented tools, tamed the winds, and much more? Certainly he
was more powerful than that goddess lying out there, opening and
closing, on the distant horizon. Certainly he could defeat even
death.

Despite numerous warnings, Māui assembled a band of warriors
for the journey to the horizon, where the eyes of the goddess
glowed red. His warrior companions of battle were all of the little
birds of the land, including the water wagtail.

When Māui and his band of birds reached the great goddess, they
found her fast asleep. Māui told the birds that he would creep into
her giant body, for only in such a manner could he slay her. He cau-
tioned the birds not to laugh, despite what they saw, until he
climbed out of her huge mouth.

The birds cried warnings, for they were afraid Māui would be
killed. He reassured them, saying that he would be killed only if
Great-Hina-of-the-Underworld were to awaken while he was inside

her. If he traveled safely through that long tunnel, she would die and human beings would become immortal. The cleverness of that fellow! He knew that he had to re-enter Hina's great womb and be born again from it, in another way, in order to reach immortality.

"Be careful!" cried the birds.

He twisted the strings of his weapons tightly around his wrist and moved closer to the goddess. He stripped off his loincloth and the skin on his hips looked as mottled and beautiful as that of a mackerel, for the tattoo marks upon him were cut with the stone of gods. Never before had Māui appeared more godlike, or seemed more human.

The hushed birds watched him crawl between Great Hina's thighs and disappear into her huge body, until only his legs stuck out. The birds tried to suppress their laughter at what really was an unusual sight, as though Māui's body had become all phallus.

The water wagtail danced about, trying not to laugh, but one merry note escaped and the goddess opened her eyes. She squeezed her legs together and Māui died right there in that place, between the thighs of Great Hina, O terrible Great Mother of Death. And there was darkness then and the crying of all birds.

Since his death, no one has ventured willingly near the horizon of Hina-Nui-ke-Pō. According to an ancient Maori proverb, "Man makes heirs, but Hina carries them off" (adapted from Luomala 1986, 1971; Reed 1963).

In the Hawaiian *Kumulipo*, we hear that Māui died while he was competing in unnamed trickery with Kāne and Kanaloa.

> He drank the muddy waters of the plain
> of Kane and Kanaloa,
> Strove by trickery,
> Around Hawaii, around Maui,
> Around Kauai, around Oahu;
> at Kahaluu is the afterbirth buried,
> at Waikane the navel string,
> He died at Hakipuu at Kualoa,
> Maui-of-the-loincloth,
> The famous demigod of the island,
> A chief indeed!
>
> (Luomala 1971)

Of course he had to die. If he had achieved immortality, he would have joined the akua and become unreachable. By dying,

Māui became an ancestor, perhaps the first ancestor in a chain of chiefs, and a link between people and the gods.

His position is similar to that of the 'aumākua, who act as a bridge between the realities of this world and that of the spirit world. Māui, however, belongs to all of the people, not only to one family. Unlike Kāne, whom he resembles in numerous ways, Māui is an ancestor. He is not far away in the heavens nor does he live on a floating island; he pulled *this* island out of the ocean and I can relate to the part of him that shares my humanity. If I can find the hero in myself, I too can pull land out of the water or find the secret for creating transforming flame.

Māui was a chief indeed. The Polynesian chiefs were the carriers of divine light for an entire group of people. They and the kāhuna were the bearers of consciousness within each generation. Whoever could chant the genealogical chants, which extended back to include all chiefs, male and female, provided the people with a connection to their own instinctual foundation.

Māui was the greatest chief. But to so limit his essence seems sacrilegious. Here my words seem inadequate, as though I were trying to understand him while still balancing on that slippery, plastic bubble. Māui did not challenge the sun *as if* it were the sun; he took it on, defied it with all of the cunning, courage, and emotional intensity such an adventure requires. He did not steal fire as though it were a fantasized interlude, he stole it because it was a necessary tool for human beings to obtain and utilize.

He defied the status quo and did what had never been done before. His adventures were an intense and emotional series of experiences. They were heroic because they were not a game, not a fantasy acted out in his head. They were real. He did what he did from his guts, and the Polynesians who shared his exploits felt the experiences in their guts also. The intestines or gut, the na'au, could provide the truth, the light of a given situation, and the head was reserved for the gods. Heroism is not a head trip.

Such heroism is repeated each time one of us claims a bit of consciousness, a measure of land, earth, air, light, or fire—some minute treasure of what had previously been sacred and kapu. We purchase that bit of awareness with a full price of guilt and conflict when we fight for it and claim it for our individual lives. The challenge is this: how do we find the way to connect with the gods, the ever-present archetypal energy, and remain human, sane, and alive?

Several years ago, there were a few moments when I almost touched the essence of Māui. In Hawai'i, the nights are like heavy velvet, much darker and more awesome than nights on the mainland. They seem to stretch forever, beyond the ocean and far above the stars. Our house faced east, toward the dawn. Early one morning, I woke up while it was still dark, and I hurried to our front lanai. I waited there, not really understanding what I waited for, listening to the morning birds begin to sing and watching for the first leg of the sun to reach above the mountain. Suddenly a streak of flame announced the golden ball to follow, and for one hushed, suspended, incredible moment, the new light felt like a victory.

6

Hina, Goddess
of the Moon

Her name is Hina. Goddess of the moon, she is moonlike in her varied aspects, phases, and moods. She is found throughout all of Polynesia and is the most widely known goddess or demigoddess there.

The stories about her are at least as ancient as those about Māui. Somewhere in a forgotten past, the two figures obviously had a common link, because she is usually found in an important role in the various stories about Māui. Sometimes she is his mother; in other tales she is his sister, wife, or grandmother. She is also Great-Hina-of-the-Underworld who finally brought him to his death. Although Hina is important in most of the Māui stories, he does not appear in a majority of the Hina tales.

She is called Hina in Hawai'i, although in other island groups her name may be pronounced Sina, Ina, or Hine. Often she is a goddess or a demigoddess whose story concerns the seminal myths of an entire culture. Sometimes she is a woman, the heroine of a romantic tale of passion and adventure. Other times she is mother, wife, or daughter of an important deity. Each of the Hinas, whatever the plot, reveals another aspect of the same symbolic core, the essence of which is lunar and feminine.

She is a multifaceted figure; the varying aspects of her personality are often expressed by numerous epithets. Each Hina is a separate personification of an underlying feminine image, which expresses itself in different ways, according to the demands of individual dramatic themes. A few examples from Hawai'i are Hina-of-the-ohia-growth, Hina-from-whom-fishes-are-born, and Hina-from-under-the-sea. There is a Hina who is the mother of the famous pig god, Kamapua'a, and another Hina who is the second wife of Wākea and the mother of the island of Moloka'i. Yet another Hina is always connected with the god Kū.

She is most often associated with the moon. In Hawaiian *mahina* means the "moon," "month," or "moonlight," and among other meanings *hina* translates as "gray." It is tempting to conjecture that the name Sina indicates a connection to the Babylonian moon god, Sin, who is a god of healing, as is Hina (Sina).

Hina-i-ka-malama (Hina-in-the-moon) is probably the same as Hina-in-the-fire, mother of Māui. As with many of the great goddesses of antiquity, the moon, fire, and fertility all belong in the domain of Hina, together with the diffused atmosphere of the night. When Māui brought the fire-making secret to his people, he had stolen the method from his mother's sacred birds. The implicit theme is that originally the secret of fire making with fire sticks (also understood as sexual generation) belonged to the mother moon goddess and that Māui's theft brought increased masculine or solar power. He, the son, representing a new and more patriarchal development in human history, stole sacred knowledge from the Great Mother Goddess. And with it, he acquired increased power over feminine spirituality and fertility.

As we know, during the early long centuries of dominance by the great goddesses of antiquity, women were seen as reflections of the feminine deities and, as a result, had enormous power as the carriers of both spirituality and fertility. When the patriarchal gods conquered those of the matriarchy, men, as reflections of the male deities, became increasingly powerful. In Western cultures today, with the first signs of re-emerging feminine power, women are once again laying claim to, and responsibility for, their own sexuality, fertility, and expression of what is spiritual in their own natures.

We think of history as a continuum and of ourselves as standing at the end of the historical line. We can only be educated by past history, however, if we are aware of what lies behind us at various earlier stages along that line. This is true psychologically also, although modern human beings have little recollection of such a psychological continuum. What did we leave behind when we took those many steps forward to our present psychological awareness? As discussed in the chapter about Māui, we can learn a great deal about the abandoned parts of ourselves when we turn our attention to mythology, where forgotten life still exists. The feminine symbolism surrounding the moon contains just such repressed life, for men as well as for women.

In most cultures, the sun is filled with masculine symbolism, as we saw in the stories about Kāne and Māui, while the moon has feminine implications. Even in those cultures in which there is a moon god instead of a moon goddess, the god usually is seen as the fertilizer of women, for example, among the Maori, where the moon god was known to be the true deity of all women and the inseminator for all new life.

For thousands of years, the sun, with its solar heroes, has represented man's deity in myth, legend, poetry, art forms, and religions. The moon has similarly represented woman's deity. It cannot be otherwise when women's very body cycles are obviously and intimately tied to lunar phases and tides. Most of us, however, women as well as men, have greatly overvalued the masculine/solar principle and have continuously undervalued or repressed the feminine/lunar principle. As a result, we are out of balance. The imbalance has become so extreme that a symbolic trip to the moon feels more mysterious and perilous than the actual trip taken by astronauts (Harding 1971).

When the night is clear and the moon is full, look up at her. It is not a man in the moon whom you see, it is Hina-i-ka-malama, only now she may also have another name. If you close your eyes halfway and focus softly, you will see her there, with her calabash at her side.

Hina worked hard when she lived on earth, arduously pounding out the finest possible tapa cloth on a long, thick board. As she worked, her family became increasingly demanding and difficult. Her husband was lazy and her sons were undisciplined. In addition, despite her semidivine origin, she had to carry her sons' excrement ever farther away from her home, and this was a daily task. At last she grew weary of her thankless work among mortals. She looked up and decided to climb to the sun, leaving her burdens below. As she climbed up her personal rainbow, however, she found the sun's heat unbearable, and finally she had to slip down her rainbow back to the ground.

That night a full moon rose into the heavens and she decided to climb up to that heavenly globe, and there find her peace. Her husband tried to hold her on the ground and they struggled, Hina crying out that she wanted to go to her new husband, the moon. Her earthly husband grabbed her leg so fiercely that it was broken. Nevertheless, Hina continued to climb and she escaped. She said strong incantations and the dark powers of the night helped her reach the silver ball in the heavens. She had packed her most precious pos-

sessions in her calabash, and she carried them with her as she limped into her new home.

Now she is called Hina-who-works-in-the-moon or sometimes she is called Lono-moku, the crippled Lono. If this second name is actually one belonging to Hina, it is interesting, because Lono is one of the major male gods. He is associated with rain, clouds, agriculture, and fertility. A similar mythological statement is found in New Zealand. The Maori identify two distinct personifications of the Moon, one is male and the other is female. The male form is Rongo (Lono in Hawai'i) and the female form is Hina (Reed 1963).

Many of the ancient moon deities, including Sin, were androgynous. In Hawai'i, too, we find a possible androgynous aspect of the moon deity and an implied connection between the moon and plants, fertility, and healing. Such connections are found in mythologies everywhere, reflecting observable phenomena in the natural world.

Hina left thankless toil behind and now appears to work contentedly in a home more to her liking. As is the case with many of the stories about her, this one strikes a responsive chord in me. Hina's moon controls the tides of emotion, as well as those of the sea. When I am overworked and overly pressured by masculine demands, most of which bombard me from within myself, the only possible freedom seems to lie in my own lunar home. I escape to my inner moon joyfully, casting off the heavy masculine expectations of society, and flee to my own place of rhythm, poetry, distilled light, and song. There I can play, and I work there too, but in the tempo of my own pulse. I can know my moods there as natural phases of my very essence as a woman and can rejoice in the relativity of all life. In that private place, I can experience once more the lunar reality where shades of silver blend into dark, as well as light, and all things somehow connect with all others.

Hina's flight is mine, and it is everywoman's journey along her own vertical path to her renewed and rightful husband-spirit. To find an inner balance, we must make that journey many times, whenever the masculine expectations become too burdensome. The demands of a woman's inner man, the animus, often bring more pressure for performance than an actual outer man, such as a flesh and blood husband or employer. Conversely, a man's anima can tyrannize him unmercifully. Inappropriate moonlike moods may overwhelm him if he does not find constructive ways to work, play, and create in a lunar, as well as solar, manner, and thus encourage the feminine principle to serve his life. Modern men, as well as women, often are afraid of the journey to the inner moon. Lunar aspects seem too close to lunacy, and moonlight reveals no certainties or consistencies. To many people it feels nebulous and terribly dangerous to trust themselves in a moonlike place.

The sun seems safer to many of us. It is the golden deity of the day, of sharp awareness, disciplined work, focused goals, and distinctions between elements. The shadows of daytime are in sharp relief against the sunlit ground. There is "yes" and "no," black and white, sinner and saint, and absolute facts. The bright victories of solar energy and science are expressions of this principle, as are armies, specializations, adversary laws, either/or logic, and nuclear blueprints for the conquest of enemies. Symbolically the sun expresses the masculine principle, the yang.

The moon, symbolizing the feminine principle, yin, is the silver deity of the night, of shadowy twilight, and the watery matrix of our human history. The domain of the lunar deity is love, intuitions, instincts, measured rhythms, and fate. It is the controller of tides, moods, and the ever changing phases of life. It controls the tides of animals and humans, as well as those of all bodies of water on earth. It reigns over tidal waves, floods, depression, lunacy, diseases of nature, and the death that naturally follows life, as the moon waxes only to wane again. The sun is constant, the moon moves through its phases endlessly. Many people like to believe that they are like the sun, but we only stand in the sunshine for a little while. Our lives are lived like phases of the moon, where the only consistency lies in change.

The Maori call her Hine. Tane fashioned her out of the red sand of Hawaiki, a mythical place of origin, after which Hawai'i is named, and he breathed life into her until she was born as Hine-hau-one, the Earth-formed-maiden. Their first child was Hine-titama, the Dawn-maiden.

After a while Tane took his daughter, the Dawn-maiden, as his wife. When the Dawn-maiden discovered that Tane was her father as well as her husband, she fled from him, down into the underworld. There she remains, and from that place she drags

Tane's children down into death. Now she is called Great-Hina-of-the-Underworld, and it is she who finally killed Māui, as she will claim all of us at our time of death.

Hina's numerous forms are moonlike in their inconsistencies. She is goddess of the moon, and similar to other Great Mother goddesses, she is also goddess of the earth, a goddess who comes up from the ocean, and also the goddess of death. She gives life and destroys it, as imaged in the moon in its phases of waning and waxing, full to dark and back to bright, moving slowly through endless deaths and rebirths.

In Hawai'i, we find her again in various translations of the *Kumulipo*, where among other aspects, she is described as a mysterious undersea woman. She, who is the womb herself, emerges from the watery womb of a hidden past. In a version of the *Kumulipo* translated by the last Hawaiian king, David Kalākaua, we read:

> Hina-[who-worked-in-the-moon] floated as a bailer,
> Was taken into the canoe, hence called "Hina the bailer,"
> Carried to the shore and put by the fire [sexual image],
> Coral insects were born, the eel was born,
> The blackstone was born, the volcanic stone was born,
> Hence she was called "Hina from whose womb came
>   various forms."
>   (Beckwith 1970:217)

The Hawaiians also attributed such procreative powers to the mother goddess Haumea. The tangle of names and ancestral feminine forms seems to emanate from the intertwined roots of a moonlit tree. The tree roots are hidden, but they have given life to symbolic expressions of something that is essentially feminine, something complex and diffused, which acts as both a creative and destructive natural force. This is the intricate weave of the web surrounding lunar symbolism.

Polynesian myths seldom clearly differentiate between the multitude of Hinas. Each, as indicated by her particular epithet, seems to reveal yet one more ramification of the same mysterious reality.

> She is Hina, the undersea woman. Long ago there was a chief of the Big Island of Hawai'i. He learned about the beautiful Hina who lived under the sea, and he desired her as his wife. His kahuna, who

was Hina's brother, instructed the chief how to lure her to shore. Hina had a husband in the underwater realm who was a carved image and also a god, and she had never seen a real man. Following the advice of his kahuna, the chief ordered many large manlike images to be carved. These were placed in a line from the ocean bottom to the shore, and then along a trail leading to the chief's house. The last image was laid upon his bed.

Thus lured, Hina followed from carved image to carved image, finally lying down next to the one on the chief's bed. Needless to say, while Hina slept, the chief replaced the wooden image with his own body, and Hina from the country under the sea became the wife of a Hawaiian chief.

Hina asked her new husband to send a man down to her former home and bring back her calabash, which she had left behind. When that was done, Hina opened her calabash and the contents flew up to the heavens in the forms of the crescent moon and the stars. This was the moon's first appearance in the sky, and it was reflected in the ocean like a paler twin. Seeing the moon's reflection, her underwater brothers came up in search of their sister. They came on giant waves that flooded the land and drowned all but Hina, the chief, and his family. These few survivors had escaped to the highest mountain on the island. After the water receded, the family returned to their homes. The destructive great flooding of the sea is called Kahinali'i (adapted from Beckwith 1970; Colum 1973).

Flood myths are found throughout the world, and may or may not describe an actual historical period of flooding. In the biblical story, the ark of Noah is an expression of the crescent moon, and the name Noah is probably a form of Nuah, a Babylonian moon goddess. Sometimes the causal factor of the mythological flooding is feminine, as seems to be the case with Hina, and other times it is masculine, as with the God of Noah. In all cases, the flood myths are a mythological expression of a threat to human structure and civilization, and most often these are brought about by a lunar deity (Harding 1971).

Dreams about flooding are common, often found in images of tidal waves, mounting water, or of being down at the bottom of the ocean.

A college student dreamed that he was in the library of the university he attended. He was seated at a table, industriously researching for his doctoral dissertation and feeling extremely pressured. Suddenly water from the adjacent ocean began to flow in through the windows; it quickly covered the floor and rose to the table tops. The frightened dreamer climbed up bookshelves, higher and higher, as the water continued to rise. Finally, in desperation, he edged along the top shelf until he reached a narrow window. Painfully squeezing through the window, he dropped to a garden below. There was no water in the small, square garden, and the dreamer collapsed on the damp earth with relief.

Naturally an interpretation of such a dream depends upon the dreamer and his or her life situation, but frequently the dream carries a meaning similar to that of a parallel myth. It describes mounting energy from unconscious water, and it suggests that the dreamer's ego may become overwhelmed. But a dream of flooding may also imply the possibility of transformation, as with the fertilization of the Nile Valley, when the Nile River overflows its banks and carries the seeds of new life to the previously arid land. This aspect of flooding and fertilization brings the healing water of life to a dry, barren existence.

On a personal level, the barren situation is experienced as depression or as a pervasive sense that one's life is meaningless. During such periods, we often feel as though the emotional color has drained out of everything, and all the world seems pale beige.

The college student who dreamed of the flood had kept himself too busy to feel anything but pressure and anxiety. He had completely dedicated himself to his books and his doctoral goal, and as a result he was emotionally out of balance. For several years he had neglected other facets of life by eating poorly, sleeping fitfully, and ignoring friends and various physical symptoms. Positioned rigidly in his head, he refused to acknowledge the signals that his instincts were sending him, until at last these same instincts threatened to overwhelm him with an emotional breakdown.

The dream informed him that he needed to make room in his life for whatever that small garden meant to him. It was a place of serenity and of all of the natural and instinctual elements that he had long ignored because they, like the garden, lay below his head and mind. The garden place could save him from a dangerous flood that threatened to drown him.

Although the story about Hina, the undersea woman, is an

ancient one, it has modern applications. The chief represents a superior personality who is the carrier of continuity for an entire society, even though a small one. At first, the story suggests that he did not have a wife, or at least not the wife he desired. This implies that the society itself was dominated by the masculine element and that the feminine principle was missing, here personified by Hina, goddess of the moon.

Hina herself had no obvious human contact, but existed in an underwater, thus unconscious, place. There she had related only to images or, as is the case in Polynesia where the deities often were represented by images, with a god. The myth may be understood to suggest that there was no human interaction between the island people and the feminine lunar spirit while she was under the sea. The kahuna performed in a priestly role, serving as a bridge between the human world and that of the spirits.

Modern parallels to the condition of most of today's societies are obvious. As previously stated, the feminine spirit has been inaccessible to most of us, women as well as men. There are exceptions, such as artists who perceive the lunar spirit as their muse, but even with them, the spirit is as wounded as was the lamed Hina who limped into the moon.

As is always the case with repressed or submerged life forces, when they finally emerge from their hidden prison, they may bring a flooding of instinctual energy in their wake. Because the energy has been trapped and uneducated about societal niceties, it has remained primitive and potentially dangerous. The still unfocused anger of women in various feminist quarters is only one example of such an outpouring. When the flooding finally occurs, our ego islands are threatened and may become overwhelmed. If we are lucky, the flooding also brings fertilization, and then life will continue, but in a new and augmented way. The moon goddess brings gifts that may be more powerful than we can handle, but she also brings the possibility of renewal and growth.

A woman dreamed that she was in a large house, with many people. Suddenly there was a loud explosion. She ran downstairs to the basement and saw water coming out of a pipe on a water storage container. The outpouring threatened to destroy the house and she did not know how to stop it. She picked up her briefcase (actually a man's briefcase that she used for her work) and threw it out the window. Immediately the water stopped flowing.

Then she went down to a subbasement and opened a door. A huge lion pounced out. Fierce and frightening, it seemed more threatening than the water. She called an emergency operator and asked for help from the police. They came and either captured or killed the lion. When she woke up, she was unable to remember how the lion was controlled. She felt safe, but also sad. Although the lion had frightened her, it was a magnificent animal.

Here the woman's own fiery, passionate nature had been imprisoned in the subbasement of her house. There was a direct connection between the man's briefcase, symbolizing her intense and single-minded involvement with her work, and the imprisonment of her own instincts. The animal, as instinctual lionlike power, had been released by the explosion and the outpouring of water, but evidently its energy was greater than she could handle at the time of the dream. She needed her own policing forces to protect her from what would have been devastating lionlike emotions.

In the Hawaiian myth, I find the particular details about Hina as the undersea woman interesting, especially the inventive twist of the plot wherein Hina followed the images of a man to the chief's bed. Women often follow images of a man, which they confuse with a real man, only to wake up to a different reality after marriage.

"He isn't who I thought he was!" they wail, and of course they are right. They confused an image with a real person, and in the emotional flood following their awakening, the marriage may drown in a sea of confusion. As discussed before, the same dynamic is true of men. Most of us fall in love with images of gods and goddesses, only to wake up with considerable discomfort to the reality of another human being. In the myth, Hina and her chiefly husband survived the flood, but the devastation was awful, and considerable rebuilding was going to be necessary.

Throughout Polynesia, Hina is found in origin stories about the coconut, together with the eel, who is often her lover. In Tonga, for example, Hina's father found her beside her bathing pool, making love with a handsome man. When her father grabbed him, Hina's lover turned into an eel and slipped into the pool. Hina's father ordered the pond to be emptied of water and when this was accomplished, the eel was cut into many pieces. The eel's head was buried and soon sprouted into the first coconut tree (Fanua 1975).

This, and closely related stories from other Pacific islands, no doubt have their inspiration from the actual appearance of a husked coconut. Each nut has three indentations at one end: two small ones that look like an eel's eyes and a larger indentation suggesting the eel's mouth. The stories all imply that the eel has godlike proportions and that Hina is the vessel that brings the new plant to birth. Together Hina and her eel-shaped, obviously phallic, lover produce a new growth that always is an essential plant in the culture expressing the myth.

Such an origin story about the coconut is not found in Hawai'i, at least not in modern Hawai'i, but we can find variations of a similar theme. Here there is Hina, mother of Māui, who lived in a cave near the Wailuku River on the island of Hawai'i. Kuna, the eel, wanted to be her lover, but she refused him. The rejected eel then tried to drown Hina while Māui was away and unable to protect his mother. Before she was overcome by the water, Hina magically called for Māui, who returned and killed the giant eel in a fierce battle, which has become legendary. Various signs of the famous battle are still visible by the shores of the Wailuku River as it flows near the city of Hilo.

She is also Hina of the Ka'ū district on the island of Hawai'i, who bore a son, Ni'auepo'o, which means "Chief-of-high-rank." The boy's father was Kū-the-leader, who had come from Kahiki, the land of the gods. When the boy was half-grown, he wanted to see his father, so Hina chanted, calling upon her ancestor, the Life-giving-coconut. A coconut sprouted in front of Hina's house and quickly grew into a tree that bore two coconuts. This was Hina's ancestor. She instructed her son to sit in the tree and to hold on to it as tightly as possible. The tree grew taller, and still taller. Hina continued to chant and the tree continued to grow, and the boy, Ni'auepo'o, clung to its branches. At last the tree bent down and formed an arched bridge to the land of the gods, Kahiki, where the boy's father lived.

Ni'auepo'o had various adventures in Kahiki. He and some other boys were swept into the ocean, but Ni'auepo'o transformed himself into an eel and saved himself and the others. Then he emerged from the ocean in his human form and was recognized by his father. Gifts were offered to the ancestor, the Life-giving-coconut,

who came up from the ocean in his eel form to accept the gifts
(adapted from Handy and Handy, with Pukui 1972).

The imagery here is interesting. Both the coconut and the eel
are forms of the god, Kū, as is the boy's father. Kū is frequently
found associated with Hina. In the Hawaiian story, Hina is pursued by Kuna (Ku-na), the eel, which is cut up or otherwise slain
by Māui. Similar motifs are found throughout Polynesia, with
the added detail of the origin of the coconut. In view of the story
about Niʻauepoʻo, I speculate that parts of the original myth
became lost in travel or with time.

The Hina–Niʻauepoʻo story provides more pieces for the mythological puzzle. The coconut, the eel, and the god Kū are all phallic elements that require the feminine element, Hina, in order to
bring something new to birth. We could turn this idea around
with equal validity and, as stated previously, observe that Hina
needs the erect masculine element in order to conceive whatever
will be born. The word *hina* means "leaning down," while the
word *kū* means "rising upright." The phallic symbolism of the
coconut tree is vividly explicit, especially as described in the
Hawaiian myth, with its two nuts growing among the leaves.
Because of their obvious resemblance to testicles, nuts are found
universally as an expression of fertility.

> O life-giving coconut
> That budded in Kahiki
> That rooted in Kahiki
> That formed a trunk in Kahiki
> That bore leaves in Kahiki
> That bore fruit in Kahiki
> That ripened in Kahiki.
> (Handy and Handy, with Pukui 1972)

This, the chant with which Hina, mother of Niʻauepoʻo, sum-
moned her Life-giving-coconut ancestor, is almost identical to
the chant with which herb pickers addressed Hina and Kū. The
herbs that were (or are) used for medicinal purposes needed the
power of Hina, as the goddess of healing, and that of Kū, the
erect, phallic inseminator. The Hawaiian traditions regarding
Hina's healing powers have a wisdom that is impressive in its
clear, universal validity.

In Hawaiian legend and practice, the lunar aspect of healing is not expressed solely by the moon goddess, but by Hina and Kū in conjunction. This might be termed the Hina–Kū constellation of the godhead. As gods, Hina and Kū are considered individual deities, each with her or his own individual functions and attributes, including that of medicine. But together, the Kū-and-Hina godhead has much broader implications and symbolism. In the godhead of duality, with its implied union of male and female, a third reality is constellated, one which may be considered the archetype of healing or of health. Kū-with-Hina, like the yang-with-yin symbol of Chinese Tao, symbolizes the balance embodied within the conjunction of opposites, with resultant harmony and health.

In Hawai'i, the realms of healing and healer, healing plant, and recuperative growth meet in the conjunction of Hina and Kū. Medicinal plants were picked with the right hand, accompanied by a prayer to Kū, and with the left hand, accompanied by a prayer to Hina. The herbs were kept separately in the two hands until they were joined with prayers to both Kū and Hina, whereupon they were crushed and given to the patient. As with various other rituals of natural or folk medicine, the plants usually were picked at night, under the auspices of lunar power.

The cool, moist night brings us sleep and restoration. Healing occurs in dark secrecy, as though the night itself were a renewing womb. Plants picked in the night, during certain prescribed periods of time and moon phase, are filled with healing potency and are associated with lunar medicine. Many of the moon deities throughout the world have been physicians.

The healing power of the moon is illustrated in the experience of a modern man. Routine laboratory tests had indicated the possibility of a serious illness. He had been asked to return for more tests in several weeks. While he was waiting for the second series of tests, he put time and energy into the condition of his body and psyche, doing his own form of meditation, soul-searching, and self-healing. He used every method he knew about, all in an effort to bring himself into balance. After a while he had the following dream:

> It's nighttime and I'm standing on the ground, looking up at a large, crescent moon shining above me. A dark line, like a taut wire, stretches down straight from the moon and touches the earth

in front of my feet. It almost seems as though the moon is com-
municating something to me, and the message fills me with peace.

When he woke up, he felt that the dream related to his health
and his efforts to heal himself, and he felt encouraged. His doctor
was surprised when subsequent tests proved negative and the
man was given a clean bill of health.

Moon symbolism is as elusive and variable as the numerous
manifestations of Hina. We know that the lunar quality may be a
creative and healing one, but we are unable to describe how such
lunar qualities operate. I have searched for the spirit of the moon,
knowing that it would bring healing and harmony. Not because
the lunar spirit brings all of life's truths, but because it has been
in eclipse for too many years. Despite my efforts, I have felt as
though the essence of the moon and the spirit of the moon goddess were too fluid to grasp. Finally, as happened when I felt
Māui's spirit in the rising sun, Hina became real to me in the
world of nature.

On July 5, 1982, there was a total eclipse of the moon, a
startlingly dramatic occurrence in Hawaiian skies. The eclipse
was impressive, and my response was even more startling to me.
I had been restless, vaguely anxious, off-balance for several days.
(Later I learned that other people had felt similar sensations.) I
had attributed my condition to overwork and to too much stress.
Like other sun worshipers, I frequently ignore my relationship to
moon tides and phases, and then I suffer from imbalance and disorientation because I have forgotten life's duality. I was prepared
for the eclipse and comprehended some of the scientific explanation for what was happening, and yet, at a more visceral level,
my reaction was absolutely primitive. I could barely breathe
while the moon was slowly devoured by a heavy shadow. A mon-
strous evil force was eating the familiar bright globe in the dark
sky and it might snuff out all of life, or so it seemed to the suddenly panicked creature who had awakened in my stomach. It
was awesome and awful. I felt cold.

Later I watched, with equal fascination, the miraculous reap-
pearance of a pale sliver of light as it grew again to full strength.
Life could start once more and there was hope for tomorrow.
Instead of laughing with joy, I wept.

The Hawaiians said about such a heavenly drama, "The moon

is consumed by the gods." For human beings who remain in touch with the passion of nature, an eclipse is a monumental occurrence. It is the moment when the sun and moon meet in conjunction, a time of fear, dread, and destruction, but it is also the precise moment when fertilization occurs which may lead to new birth.

That night I had connected with ancient moon mysteries for the first time. Altogether it was a night of change for me and it made a qualitative difference in my perception of myself and of my relationship to my own inner moon. A drama that was being enacted within my psyche had found itself in projection in the heavenly theater. Suddenly I knew that it was time for me to begin to move out of the bright glare of the sun.

Hina. Can you grasp her? I am not quite able to do so, and it is likely that I never will. I might as well try to hold on to a moonbeam or fully describe the essence of the feminine spirit. Like a muse, Hina leads ever onward, seldom motionless long enough to be embraced. It does not matter what I call her: goddess, muse, moon, or mahina. She is not me, certainly not in my all too human existence, but I partake of her essence in my own nature, wherein she remains elusive, shadowed, and valid.

> For I harbor shimmered silver shades
> in the shadows of my too bright days.
> Secret waters of sheltering tides
> hide lunar mysteries, darkened now,
> but blooming pearly harvest there.

7

Miraculous
Menehune

Quick! Turn around! See that little guy behind the tree! It's a Menehune, I know it is, because he just disappeared when I blinked my eyes!

I have a special fondness for the Menehune, because they led me to my interest in Hawaiian mythology. During our first trip to Hawai'i, my husband and I had been enjoying the usual visitor activities on Kaua'i, and we set out one day for the Menehune Fish Pond. We got lost and ended up at a tourist attraction called The Menehune Gardens. A delightful Hawaiian woman guided us through lush tropical gardens, pointing out various plants and trees while telling a few stories. During a brief rainfall, we took shelter under a banana tree and I asked her about the Menehune.

She said they were hardworking little people who toiled only at night and had built some unusual stone constructions on the islands. She added that they had accomplished marvelous works, but had left Hawai'i because they were displeased with the Hawaiians. Perhaps this was her usual remark invented to entertain tourists, because never again did I hear such a reason given for the Menehune departure. Her statement caught my interest, however, and I wondered if the mythological Menehune represented some aspect of Hawaiian culture that was absent in contemporary Hawai'i.

After we returned to the mainland, I continued to speculate about the mysterious Menehune. I am still not sure what was so intriguing, but a hidden bait lured me to start looking for information about them. One book led to another, as the Menehune started me on a trail marked by mythological figures such as Pele, her sisters, and then to Hina and Māui. Before I realized what was happening, I was waist deep in material about Polynesia. Evidently the Menehune truly can perform miraculous tasks, although not necessarily those requested. The small, creative spirits popped into my life and stayed around long enough to shake me up, turn me around, and lead me on to unforeseen adventures.

It is the "real" Menehune that I am talking about, not the cute, pixielike figures that topple from souvenir shelves in Waikīkī. I mean the little folk who made such extraordinary stonework throughout the Hawaiian Islands. They built waterways, fishponds, roads, and temples, the construction of which is superior to the stonework done by Hawaiians in historical periods. They are purported to have built much more than the facts justify, but exaggeration is an integral part of the mythology surrounding them. Most Menehune seem to have vanished with the arrival of the foreigners, although occasional Menehune sightings have continued until recently.

The Menehune have been described in various ways. According to one source, they are two or three feet in height, very thickset and strong, and quite hairy, with ugly, red faces. Incidentally, the Menehune are not the only little people who live or lived in Hawai'i. One way not to confuse a Menehune with a Mū, or a Wā, or even a Wao, is to notice the abdomen. The abdomens of Menehune are extremely distended, and those of the Mū, for example, are round (Luomala 1971).

A great deal has been written about the Menehune, some of it scholarly, but much of it rather tongue-in-cheek fillers for tourist publications. Such stories provide local interest, without taxing the minds of vacationing visitors. In addition, of course, Menehune are natural subjects for illustrated children's books. Children love to hear about people as small as they, who have magical power over the adult community. In all quarters, interest remains high about the little people, along with occasional speculation as to their origin and actual place in Hawaiian history. It is possible that they were the first kama'āina, or native born, of Hawai'i, but nobody knows for sure. There are at least five traditional versions of their origin and an equal number of reasons given for their departure.

One scholar compiled a list of twenty-two similar native beliefs about various little people of Oceania and demonstrated that the Menehune shared characteristics with their kinfolk throughout the Pacific region (Luomala 1971). She finally equated the Menehune with lower-class workers on other Pacific islands, such as the workers of Tahiti who were called *mana-hune*. Her thesis is that the mythological Menehune are real only in the context of folk beliefs and mythology and that they never actually existed as they have been described. They were invent-ed, she states, by storytellers who had assimilated other stories about other little people. There are those who disagree with her, and they point to the amazing stonework as proof of Menehune reality.

Tempting though it is, I am not going to enter into the Mene-hune controversy, which continues to make good reading. Were they real people? If so, who were they? Why did they leave Hawai'i? Why are most of the stories about them localized on Kaua'i, and to a lesser extent on O'ahu?

The questions are fun to juggle, but I am much more interested in the Menehune as a psychological phenomenon. I start from the premise that the Menehune, historical or mythical or both, reflect a universal behavior pattern that operates inside full-size people, if not within the tiny folk hiding behind trees. In that sense, the Menehune certainly are "real." There is no other valid reason for their continued popularity.

The earliest reference to the Menehune that Luomala found as a written or translated manuscript is dated 1885. It is a legend about Pi, a Hawaiian man who is also found in other Menehune stories; like a large number of Menehune tales, the story takes place on Kaua'i.

Pi was related to the Menehune. He lived at Hulā'ia when the chief of that place was building a large bank for a taro patch in order to separate it from a river. Although the chief and his men had been working on the project for a long time, the task was still unfin-ished. The men worked hard, and for their labor they received pay-ment of food, fish, tapa, and loincloths.

Pi, on the other hand, received no food or tapa cloth, because he did no work. It was said that he was very lazy. When Pi's children complained that they were hungry, Pi's wife scolded her husband and told him to start working so that their children would have food to eat.

Pi listened to her, but he did not go to work like the other men. Instead, he went to the upland and gathered taro to cook. After it was cooked, he divided it into as many bundles as there were Menehune he wanted to come to his aid. He put the bundles of food up on the branches of a tree and carried the tree to the place where

the chief and his men had been working. It is said that this was the first time Pi ever did any work.

Pi was not disappointed. During the night, the Menehune came to that place and, standing in a row, they handed stones from one little fellow to another, until they had built a wonderful wall. In the morning it was done. When it was discovered that Pi and his Menehune relatives had finished the job, the chief sent a great deal of fish and bundles of tapa cloth to Pi's house. Pi did not share these things with the other men, because they had never shared their gifts with him.

When Ola, the high chief of the area, heard about the amazing work Pi had finished in one night, he sent for him. Ola and his men had been working on a waterway, but it was difficult to finish. Again Pi solicited his relatives, the Menehune, and this time he gave each of them a shrimp in addition to the cooked taro. Each Menehune liked to have a separate shrimp to eat, not liking to divide food into many pieces. The shrimp must have pleased the Menehune, because they came to Pi's aid again. In the course of one night, they completed the wonderful waterway, the Menehune Ditch. Parts of the waterway are still visible on the island of Kaua'i (adapted from Luomala 1971).

The tone of the translated legend is not that of the breezy, coy, and sometimes charming, Menehune stories found today in travel booklets or in children's books. It does not claim to be absolutely factual, but one can sense a mythological seriousness in the legend about Pi and his relatives, the Menehune gods.

Evidently there were women and children among the Menehune, but little is said about them, except once or twice as secondary figures. I have yet to run across a claim that someone has seen a female Menehune, although there are numerous accounts of male Menehune encountered in various localities. One of the legendary reasons given for the Menehune's departure from Hawai'i is that they were marrying too many Hawaiian women, no doubt thus diluting the purity of the race. Their chief ordered an immediate exit from the Hawaiian Islands, insisting that the Menehune husbands must leave their Hawaiian wives behind. If the little men found it necessary to marry outside their own clans, we might assume a shortage of Menehune women.

On the other hand, it is more than possible that the female Menehune were irrelevant to the basic mythological core. In such a case, the little people are to be understood as small masculine gods of some sort who are not differentiated, because rarely does the name of an individual Menehune appear as part of a story. They belong to the innumerable spirits, which the Hawaiians count by the forties, the four hundreds, four thousands, and the four hundred thousands. Prayers were invoked to them en masse to assure that not one was skipped and insulted. Mythologically and psychologically they operate at such a deep place in the human psyche that no one Menehune appears to be different from any other. In fact, their very uniformity is an outstanding characteristic.

The closer any unconscious element moves toward human awareness, the more individualized and differentiated it becomes. The Menehune, therefore, can be seen as operating at an early level of human development. This may account for their disappearance from the Islands, or at least for the perception of them as existing in an earlier era. The only characteristics that separate the little people from each other are those connected with their work. Reportedly Menehune were specialists in their various crafts and trades, and a division of labor seems to have been their style.

They resemble the little people in other mythologies everywhere. Leprechauns come to mind, as do all the other diminutive spirits who interact with those of us of larger dimensions. The little ones work only at night and disappear once they have completed a seemingly impossible task, or when the sun first rises above the horizon, whichever comes first. During the night, they have somehow separated the grains, seeds, pins, or needles; they have fixed a hundred pairs of shoes; they have cleaned the house or barn; or they have built a fishpond or waterway before dawn.

Various sources describe the Menehune as working in the deepest dark of night, within *Pō*. As discussed previously, from a psychological viewpoint, Pō can also be understood as an expression for the dark realm within us, the unconscious psyche. The Menehune within us do their work unseen, but unlike many dreams, which tend to fade in the daylight, the finished products of the little people can be grasped in the morning—if we move quickly enough. Millions of these little Somethings work busily at night, outside our illuminated awareness, and then they present us with amazing surprises when we rub the sleep out of our eyes.

And yet the stories tell us that they do not work for just anyone. They worked for Pi because he was a relative, which means that he had a relationship with them, and because he prepared food for them. Another popular story concerns a boy named Laka. (This is a hero, not the goddess of hula with the same name.)

> Laka was brought up by his grandmother on the island of Maui. Before he was born, his father had gone to get a birth gift for his unborn child and had never returned. When the other children ridiculed Laka because he had no father, the young hero decided to find his father or his father's bones. But to embark upon such an adventure, Laka first needed a canoe.
>
> Following his grandmother's advice, Laka cut down a suitable tree. The next day, when he returned to where he had left the log, he found it upright; it was once again a tree planted in the ground. This happened several times. Each day Laka chopped down the tree, only to find it standing upright and replanted when he returned the following morning.
>
> Again his grandmother gave him advice. This time she told him to hide in a hole during the night and see if he could discover who was playing such tricks on him. That night he watched as the little people of the forest, the Menehune, chattered among themselves as they started to resurrect the fallen tree. He grabbed two of the Menehune leaders and refused to let them go until they promised to build him a canoe. He prepared food for them and, following their directions, he constructed a canoe shed beside the ocean.
>
> Evidently he satisfied them, because the Menehune built a fine canoe and carried it down to the ocean, putting it into the canoe shed. All of this was accomplished in one night. Laka set forth in the canoe and found his father's bones on the island of Hawai'i. After several heroic adventures, he returned his father's bones to Maui and hid them in a cave, thus giving proper respect to the father he had never seen.

Usually it is true that one must feed the Menehune in order to obtain their help. Psychologically this means that we must give them nourishment and energy. Both Pi and Laka worked conscientiously in the preparation of the food. I understand this to mean that the little people will help us, but only after we have done a certain amount of preparation ourselves. Each part of our work must be earnest and complete, each separate step regarded seriously, because all the stories inform us that Menehune do not like a large fish that has been divided into pieces. Each worker requires his individual shrimp or bundle of taro.

Menehune share characteristics with little people found all over the world, dating from antiquity to the present time. There is a long list of such spirits, including dwarfs, elves, gnomes, brownies, pixies, leprechauns, thumblings (like Tom Thumb), and dactyli (which means fingers). As with the Menehune, the thumblings and the dactyl-fingers are masculine figures, and so are the ancient gnomes. These are all small, strong, and potent. Like the phallus, they work in the dark and from that place, they may produce new life. They are all personifications of certain creative forces, of which the phallus is a symbol and the penis is a physiological organ.

Adjectives such as *clever, creative, magical,* and *mischievous* are attached to the diminutive populations. Most, including the Menehune, are understood to be industrious earth gods who produce miraculous work, usually as smiths or craftsmen. Inasmuch as early Hawaiian crafts often involved the use of stone or wood, it is not surprising that these crafts were credited to Menehune also. However, there are no remaining wooden pieces, such as Laka's canoe, to which we can point as remnants of Menehune industry.

Psychologically we can understand the little people as personifications of creative impulses that come to us from our own unseen places. They personify the hidden forces of nature, both in the outer world and within our own human nature. These impulses, like the Menehune, work best in the dark, and we are well advised not to watch them as they work. Several stories illustrate how Menehune are capable of turning prying humans into stone.

On a personal level, I understand this to mean that creative impulses or ideas need a dark womb in which to grow to full term. Such a process needs to develop without witness. If we dig up the ground to see how a seed is flourishing, we might kill it before it reaches the earth's surface. If we expose a creative impulse to the bright light of rational evaluation during its gestation period, it may become petrified.

Any kind of creative process needs to grow first in darkness. Numerous creative projects have slipped through artists' fingers because they spoke about them too soon. The projects or ideas were handled roughly when what they required was a private corner in which to mellow and ripen.

In this era of frankness, where discussion of feelings and constant open communication is held as a supreme virtue, creative relationships have suffered a similar aborted fate. Some issues need to be discussed with another person in order to clarify misunderstandings, but other matters should not be discussed, at least not prematurely. They need to be kept in a quiet corner until they have matured sufficiently to be born as new possibilities. There are secrets of the soul, and these must stay in a private place so that they can work their changes upon us. As Hawaiians have known, words can be powerful and may produce negative, as well as positive, effects once they are expressed.

Menehune may be seen as certain creative thoughts or ideas that pop into our minds unbidden. They are "amoral" in the sense that our usual value system and mind set is irrelevant to their appearance. Most of us have had the experience of "sleeping on a problem." We worry and struggle, trying to figure out the way to do something or solve a knotty dilemma, and then we wake up in the morning with an unexpected solution. Often it is exactly the right answer. Perhaps the Menehune did the work while we were asleep.

Evidently we have a responsibility in that solution also. It seems important that first we work and struggle with the problem. That would be the food for the little people. A broad concept or vision is only the starting place. The Menehune seem to have fussy appetites, so the food takes a special kind of preparation. Many a potentially creative artist has carried an image around in his or her head for a lifetime, never undertaking the necessary tasks to actualize the vision. Perfection is a seductive idea. It presents us with an image that is humanly impossible to duplicate. Unfortunately, some people hold on to the perfect image and leave the necessary work undone just because the results may be imperfect. It is as though the whole fish is so beautiful in its entirety that the person cannot bear to cut into it; while at the same time, he or she rejects a shrimp as too small to be of value.

Once the answer or idea has popped into our heads, we must humanize the work that was done during the night. We must make a conscious decision as to whether it is the proper solution to a particular human dilemma or is an appropriate idea or vision. If it is, we need to actualize it, give it form. This is our human responsibility, because gifts from the little people have a way of disappearing quickly. These gifts may seem small and unimportant, and we may not recognize their value until we add our own labor to what has been presented to us from the nightworld.

Robert Louis Stevenson writes about the little people, also referring to them as his "Brownies." He speaks of their assistance when he begins to worry about a story, of how they stir themselves on the same quest and labor for him all night long. They set before his eyes "truncheons of tales upon their lighted theater. . . . (They) do one half my work for me when I am fast asleep, and in all human likelihood, do the rest for me as well, when I am wide awake and fondly suppose I do it myself."

Stevenson gives credit to the little people for much of the plot of *The Strange Case of Dr. Jekyll and Mr. Hyde*, which, he says, initially appeared before his eyes in a dream. He adds that the further development of his story was greatly aided by his little helpers, his Brownies. With the same intuitive grasp of unconscious processes with which he wrote many of his articles and stories, Stevenson obviously understood the position of his ego in relation to the hidden forces stirring about in his inner home (Woods and Greenhouse 1974:51–56). All creative people seem to have an inkling of such unseen helpers.

The night before I began to write this chapter, I had a relevant dream. I had been thinking about the Menehune, and, although I had collected quite a bit of information about them, I had a gnawing sense that something important was missing. I was right. The dream had two parts:

First it is nighttime and I am standing at the seashore, looking at the ocean. As I watch the tides regularly flowing in and out, I notice two large, triangular stone constructions, rather like pyramids. They stand exactly at the shoreline, and when the tide comes in, the stoneworks are covered with water. When the tide recedes, they are exposed.

Then it is daytime and I am leading a workshop which has the Menehune as its topic for discussion. Four or five women are in the group, and we find a private place in which to sit in a circle. One of the women is someone I actually know in my waking life. (Mary, as I shall call her, is married to a creative man, but she herself is conventional and rigidly judgmental. In the dream, she had come to me previously for counseling, although she has never done so in reality).

I speak with the women about the Menehune, repeating some of the information I have collected. Suddenly I realize that Mary needs to understand something about the Menehune that is unexpected and new, so that the little people can touch her as deeply as they have touched me. But what can I say to her? I am wondering about this as I wake up.

When I thought about the dream in the morning, I recognized Mary as a conventional part of myself, set in her ways and closed to whatever creative impulses might come unbidden. Mary is married to a creative man, however, so those aspects of her must be hidden, finding themselves only in a projection upon her husband. In the dream, her husband had sent her to me for counseling, so evidently I needed to do some inner work with the Mary in myself who has tunnel vision.

The Mary-in-me is an aspect of what Jung has termed a *shadow* figure within my own psyche. In my dream, Mary appeared as a personification of an unknown element in my own inner house. Inasmuch as she showed up as a member of the workshop, I can assume that I needed to acknowledge her as an essential part of my potential totality. I needed to work with her. Mary, and other such hidden or shadowy aspects of my total personality, often appear as characters in my dreams, as they do in everyone's dreams. For women, such shadow dream figures are female; in the dreams of men, they are male.

The first part of my dream, wherein I stood at the shoreline, seemed to come from a deeper level. It had a numinous quality and seemed almost completely mythological. For obvious reasons, I associated the stonework with the Menehune and sensed that they stood as silent images at the threshold of the vast waters of the communal unconscious. This was the message for the Mary-in-myself. The pyramids both guard the barrier and reveal themselves, depending upon the rhythm of the tides, and if we watch them long enough, we will be able to witness what has been accomplished. The dream seemed to indicate a way I could proceed; perhaps the tide was right. Did the Menehune send me the dream?

Menehune represent a sudden appearance of psychic energy, sometimes called *libido*, in certain creative forms. They express a particular aspect of the masculine principle, one that is made up of many small elements, but one that is extremely powerful. It is appropriate that they helped Laka in his quest to find his father. Because he was raised by his grandmother, Laka needed his father or the paternal bones (which held the father spirit) in order to become a man himself. Men need to find the father principle within themselves so that they can leave the world of the mother and utilize their own masculine strength in the larger society.

Man or woman, we all need such masculine energy, and when it comes to us from the night, it may have creative possibilities. At such times, often indicated by a dream, it is as though a new idea is seeded within the womb of a person's mind. Like sperm, the tiny Menehune gods are numerous beyond count so that life may continue to re-create itself, despite obstacles and regressive tendencies.

Psychological insemination is necessary for any creative activity. People who work creatively are those who are most aware of the unfamiliar elements that suddenly jump through the windows of their lives. Indeed, they count on such invasions and may enact various rituals to activate them. When the Menehune spirits do not appear, the creative person experiences a so-called creative block and feels stranded and increasingly uneasy.

When we speak of a creative person, too often we assume that she or he somehow "possesses" a creative spark that facilitates creative actions and products. In reality, this is not the case. Instead, the individual has a particular closeness to the sparks which fly across the universe, a receptiveness to the new, untried, unbidden, or unique elements which come his or her way.

The goddess Laka sends her divine sparks into the bodies of the traditional hula dancers, so that her spirit may be danced through them. But first the dancers must cleanse themselves and pray. Their prayers are an essential aspect of the necessary rituals that channel energy from dancer to transpersonal forces, so that in return, the mana will infuse the human being. This is an equal relationship. The dancers have worked, prayed, and cleansed themselves into receptive and purified attitudes. Then, if the dancers are in harmony with the demands of the divine pattern, the goddess will enter and join with the supplicants to produce the dance. Such a relationship is well known to people who are able to produce creative work.

The first line of a poem pops into the poet's mind, often induced by a particular emotional state such as sadness or love. More lines and images solidify as the poet turns the line around and around, observing it from all angles. Once the words begin to appear, the creative thrust, the yang principle, is activated. Now is the time for work and polish, rework and rewrite, all of which is active movement toward a goal. Gradually the poet, artist, or artisan discovers the time to be receptive and the time to be active. The tides flow in and cover the shore, then the tides ebb and the stonework is revealed.

The receptivity of the creative act is not to be confused with passivity. To be receptive means to hold oneself alive and open, waiting to hear what wants to be heard and to see what wants to be envisioned: to work while waiting; to have a door in one's psychological house through which the Menehune may enter at night; to have a roof in that house through which rain, as the living water of life, may penetrate; to wait for the silver spear of moonlight to enter a window and impregnate.

This may be a time of fear. Darkness is all around and we must stand on the narrow threshold of what is known, while facing the unknown. It takes courage to stand there and stare into what appears as emptiness or chaos, while waiting. It takes strength to hold the fear and not be overwhelmed by it, not to turn back to the familiar light of yesterday. Facing tomorrow creatively requires a steadfast devotion to those sparks that appear out of the night. Perhaps it is for this reason that artists, when true to their own visions, are the heralds of the future.

A young artist once spoke to me about the images that bombard him and with which he tries to connect as he casts them into metal forms. He described the way he captures the images, first by concentrating upon them, then drawing them, and later building them into three-dimensional models. This takes a tremendous amount of time and energy, and in his case, considerable personal sacrifice. Unless he engages in such a continuous encounter, however, he begins to feel rather "crazy," as he expressed it.

Such feelings are a common experience during states of creative tension. I suspect they come from the chaotic stirrings of psychic energy, which produce the images, and that they represent an inner demand for a creative encounter. Without such an encounter, the energy remains stirred up and will find another channel for release. That other channel may not be a desirable one; in fact, an alternative flow of energy may have a negative effect on human life and values. Energy is neither positive nor negative, it simply *is*, and its potential for good or ill depends upon the conduit provided for its release.

The process of relating to the images that come from the unconscious psyche is called *imagination*. Imagination is not a passive state like daydreaming, which rarely accomplishes anything constructive. Rather, imagination is an active process, requiring participation with the images that have come to us as gifts. The struggle with those images demands the utilization of our uniquely human ability to undertake such participation.

I asked the young artist how the initially strong visual images came to him. He replied, "Oh, they always come in through the back door."

Menehune, no doubt, were scurrying about in his back yard while he was asleep. He had been hospitable toward the helpful little people, who need to be constantly rewarded for their efforts. In accord with the rules of hospitality, he had maintained his part of the unspoken bargain. He had gone as far as possible during the daytime hours, preparing food for the little people and appreciating their toil when he received their gifts. As a vital contribution to their mutual enterprise, he worked with devotion as he completed the work begun by his little helpers.

Menehune are liable to pop up anywhere, and we must be alert to their comings and goings. As mentioned, my first encounter with the Menehune was under a banana tree. It was an interesting place for our initial meeting, because their close cousins the Mū are called *Mū-ʻai-maiʻa* (Banana-eating-Mū). Various legends and myths imply that the Hawaiians regarded wild bananas as primordial and thus, in terms of originating in mythological time, associated with an ancient race, such as the Mū, and perhaps by extension with the other little people also. Had some member of a diminutive ʻohana caused me to misread the tourist book so that I ended up under a banana tree, beginning an entirely new phase of my life? Anything is possible when one is dealing with such amazing little spirits.

Menehune work for all of us, not just artists and artisans. We would make a serious mistake if we were to confuse the artistic product, or even the artist or artisan, with the creative process. There is a certain creative attitude which does not necessarily produce a canoe, a stone wall, a hula chant, a painting, or a poem. It is rather an attitude which may lead to a creative relationship with another person and with one's own life. As such, it is an attitude leading to intrinsic growth and in the direction of individual wholeness. In this sense, we may also create ourselves.

Menehune are a multitude of spirits, which Hawaiians count by the hundreds of thousands, but there are others behind them. These are the primary gods and goddesses who have consolidated the divine energy into one focused force. There is Kāne, the creator, symbolized by the phallic stones which were his altars. There is Kū, the erect, who signifies the upright masculine principle. There is Lono, god of fertility, who spreads his seed over the earth and brings his potency to each harvest. And there is Kanaloa, one of whose forms is the very banana tree that changed my life.

Behind these powerful masculine spirits, we will discover the awesome power of the mother goddesses, who themselves are funnels for the power of the Great Mother. Whatever lies behind her is still without name. All of these spirits bring the mana that pounds upon our windows and doors, demanding entrance into our lives.

It is easier to deal with the little people than with the primary godlike forces. As is true with other little people around the world, the Menehune are earth spirits with whom one may have a sensible dialogue in everyday language. They are accessible to us, but we must remember that they are fingers or children of the Mother herself. If we listen and are able to learn, they will help us recognize the limitations of the houses into which we have built ourselves. Mother Nature will have her due, whether we will it or not, and it is certainly easier to move willingly than unwillingly.

So I, for one, intend to tie the shrimp and taro into little bundles and place them in a tree outside my house. I shall close my eyes tightly when I go to sleep, knowing that I can wake up early in the morning and discover what gifts the Menehune have left for me with the new day. It seems to me that we human beings need every bit of help we can get.

O the four thousand gods,
The forty thousand gods,
The four hundred thousand gods,
The file of gods,
The assembly of gods!
O gods of these woods,
Of the mountain,
And the knoll,
At the water-dam,
Oh, come!

(Luomala 1971:32)

8

Woman
of the Pit

The god is at work in the hills;
She has fired the plain oven-hot;
The forest-fringe of the pit is aflame;
Fire-tongues, fire-globes, that sway in the wind—
The fierce bitter breath of the Goddess!
(Emerson 1978:166–167)

My INITIAL exposure to Madame Pele's power was impressive. It was during the 1977 eruption, which I watched on a television screen from the safety of my living room. The volcano Kīlauea erupted on the Big Island of Hawai'i, more than two hundred miles from our home on O'ahu, but our house was soon dusted with fine, gray, volcanic ash. Fascinated, I watched the red lava gobble up hundreds of acres of land. People were evacuated from their homes as far away as the Kalapana area, a coastal community many miles from the volcano; the steaming lava was expected to reach them within hours. The people in Kalapana were remarkably calm. Not passive, but calm.

I now know that various prayers, rituals, and offerings had been performed in Kalapana. The people have an ancient wisdom about ways to appease the fiery goddess, and so they were not surprised when the lava flow stopped short of their homes by only three-fourths of a mile. It had happened in such a way before. Pele's people have learned how to reckon with the fire goddess, that passionate Woman of the Pit.

The first time I drove along the Chain of Craters Road, which runs from the volcano to the sea, it had been reopened for only a few months. Its previous course had been buried under thousands of tons of volcanic rock and lava from various eruptions.

Driving between the smaller craters and the alternating waves of smooth and rippled hardened lava was like cruising through an ocean of petrified life. Where trees had once flourished on the broad slopes of the mountain, now ghostly skeletons raised stumped arms to the sky, as if they were beseeching mercy from the goddess. It reminded me of an ancient Hawaiian chant about Pele.

> She comes first to the top of the mountain
> Young and beautiful, dancing in all her glory.
> Then she sleeps, becomes old and ugly,
> Moves through the hidden ways of the mountain
> To come out near the seashore—
> Angry and capable of great destruction.
> (McBride 1972:30)

Since 1977 the volcano has erupted frequently. Even as I write, pressure is building up again inside the fire pit and another eruption is expected soon. The episodes have different patterns, but always there is the display of enormous power and I, among others, continue to react with awe. With each eruption, one more chapter is added to the local Pele lore. Nowhere else in the world does volcanic mythology exist as it does in Hawai'i, and Pele is the central figure of those myths. She is a singularly explosive, colorful, and impassioned goddess and may well be the most dramatic figure presently found in mythology anywhere.

Pele is still alive in Hawai'i, perhaps less so on O'ahu than on the Big Island, but she remains a force with which to reckon. She is found in stories and chants; and she moves on the land, rules from within her crater, and walks along paths, dark roads, and lonely beaches. I have yet to see her myself, but many others claim to have met her in one of her two basic forms: fire or human.

In human form, she is reported to appear as a lovely young woman or an ugly and weathered hag. According to some legends, Pele appears to someone in one of her human forms shortly before a major volcanic eruption. This serves as a warning to watch the volcano and be careful. If Pele is dressed in red, it is a clear warning of a coming eruption. If she is dressed in white, then the warning may refer to an approaching illness. Occasionally she has been seen as a woman engulfed in flames or perhaps as a leaping flame that is shaped like a woman. Sometimes she appears alone, other times she is accompanied by a white dog or by her favorite sister, the young Hiʻiaka-i-ka-poli-o-Pele (Hiʻiaka-in-the-bosom-of-Pele).

One day in 1984, Kīlauea erupted simultaneously with Mauna Loa, the world's largest active volcano. Mauna Loa also is within Pele's domain, as are all the volcanoes in Hawaiʻi, and the joint display of fireworks was doubly impressive. The eruption was accompanied by an earthquake, loud noises, a snowfall on Mauna Loa, and a mysterious white light that streaked across the sky between the two volcanoes. The white light appeared just as Kīlauea ended its one day eruption, so many people believed that the light was Pele, traveling as a fireball back from Kīlauea to Mauna Loa.

In whatever form or at whatever place Pele is encountered, she must be treated with respect. A wrinkled hag walking alone along the highway must be given a ride, even if she repays the courtesy by disappearing from the back seat of the car. Recently I heard a personal account about such an old woman, accompanied by a white dog, who disappeared as soon as my informant gave her a requested cigarette. Various tales are told about Pele, disguised as a hungry beggar and asking for food. If her requests are refused, the offense is swiftly punished by flowing lava or another disaster. Pele may be met anywhere, at any time, and serious problems can follow quickly on the heels of disrespect for the mighty goddess. She is Pele, sacred hewer-of-land.

Among Hawaiians she is often called Tūtū (Grandmother) Pele, and is spoken about with a unique combination of affection, fear, and reverence. She is almost like a member of the family, especially for those Hawaiians who can claim her or one of her relatives as an ʻaumakua. ʻAumakua or not, Pele remains a presence on these islands, and caution is advised in any dealings with her.

It is likely that such a careful response to the goddess is mild compared to what she must have evoked during an earlier era. There must have been a time, not long ago, when the very thought of the great goddess brought profound emotions, for then her power was considerably stronger. Then the archetypal image and energy, which Pele personifies as a local representative of the Great Mother, was still completely projected out to where the Woman of the Pit ruled absolutely. Today she is no longer Great

Mother, but Grandmother or Tūtū, and closer in kinship to her people. Now much, although certainly not all, of her potency has dropped into the pit of darkness within each of us.

I understand such Pele energy and power. Although I have not met the fire goddess on the beach or along a darkened road, I encounter her frequently in other places. Not only is Pele still alive within the hearts of the Hawaiians, but I recognize her elemental passion whenever it erupts from within me or from the dark pit-world of others. Then the violence of the Pele passion threatens everything and everyone within reach of its fiery thrust. Analogous to the volcanoes, which one ignores at one's peril, the inner volcano goddess remains a force with which we must deal cautiously.

Hers is not a two-dimensional image to be captured by camera or brush stroke, but an elemental core of untamed energy that is bigger than any human life or comprehension. It explodes in a fiery fountain of primitive power, demanding respect and attention. Few of us, however, know how to cope with her passion or how to find the necessary rituals and sacrifices that would halt her destructive flow of lava. As is often the case, a closer look at the mythological field surrounding the volcanoes may give us new understanding about ourselves.

Pele is sometimes called *akua malihini* (foreign god). According to legends, she was born in a faraway land, sometimes referred to as Kahiki. Some say that Pele was driven out of her original home by her older sister, whose husband she had stolen. This sister was a goddess of the sea and pursued Pele with tidal waves and great floods all the way to Hawai'i.

Other legends claim that Pele simply longed to travel, and tucking her little sister, Hi'iaka-i-ka-poli-o-Pele, under her arm, she set off with various members of her family. Another version relates that in her original home, Pele was an apprentice to Lono-makua, a fire god. One day, in his absence, she destroyed important land with flames. As a result of the fire, her sister, the goddess of the sea, pursued her.

Hawaiian images are rich with symbolic implications. This is well illustrated by the figure of Lono-makua, who is known as Pele's fire-keeper and is represented by the fire sticks, which themselves symbolize fertilization, sexuality, and various other aspects of fire and passion. It is likely that the fire Pele started in her homeland relates to the sexual passion and fertility that she brought with her to Hawai'i.

After arriving at the Hawaiian archipelago by way of the north-western shoals, Pele stopped at various islands, searching for the ideal new home for her family of fire deities. She traveled across the Hawaiian chain in an eastern direction—Niʻihau, Kauaʻi, Oʻahu, and so on—stopping at each island and testing what are now extinct or inactive volcanoes, until she reached the island of Hawaiʻi. There she climbed to Kīlauea Crater and made her home in the Halemaʻumaʻu fire pit. Her legendary journey across Hawaiʻi was in the sequential order of the islands' creation by volcanic action.

There are numerous legends that illuminate the explosive and unpredictable aspects of Pele's character. Many of these are accounts of her destruction of lovers or rivals, either sexual or athletic, by encasement in mounds of molten lava. It was said that she was as "fiery and impetuous as her own volcano, and almost as elemental in her passions; it was dangerous to cross her; it was almost as dangerous to be loved by her" (Andersen 1969:267). The following legend is a typical example.

Two symmetrical mounds lie at the end of a tract of old lava, which stretches for several miles. These are called the Hills of Pele. The land there is called Kahuku, and although it is now desolate and barren, once it was lushly fertile terrain. There were sugarcane fields, taro beds, and a multitude of bright flowers and trees. There were villages also, filled with many people who supported the wealthy chiefs of Kahuku.

Two of these chiefs were young and handsome. They both excelled in the athletic feats that were the main royal diversion in those days. Wherever a hillside was covered with grass and sloped properly, sled races were the favorite sport. Courageous young men and women competed with energetic skill, as they sped down the hills on their sleds.

Pele delighted in sledding and often appeared among the young people in the form of a beautiful and athletic chiefess. One day she carried her sled to Kahuku and competed with the other women, easily surpassing them in grace and daring. The two handsome young chiefs challenged her to compete with them. Days passed as the three raced together and evidently indulged in other passions also. The men were captivated by the charms of the goddess and vied with each other in lovemaking, as well as sledding.

At last the men became suspicious of their companion. Her passion was fitful and capricious, sometimes burning with raging fire and often igniting into fury at the slightest provocation. Soon the chiefs were warned that the stranger might be Pele from the other side of the island, she who carried control of underworld flames wherever she went.

The chiefs compared their experiences and then began to withdraw from the stranger. But Pele would not let them escape. She continually called them to sport with her. Now the grass began to die, the soil became warm, and the heat grew increasingly intense. Slight earthquakes were felt. The ocean was restless, casting ever stronger waves against the shore.

As the chiefs became afraid, Pele was overcome with anger and her appearance changed. Her hair floated in tangled webs, heated by the movement of hot winds. Her limbs shone as if encased in fire, her eyes blazed like lightning, and her breath spilled forth in volumes of smoke. The men rushed away from her in voiceless terror.

Pele stamped the ground furiously. Earthquakes cracked the land and an awful flood of fiery lava broke from the underworld, sweeping over Kahuku. The goddess rode on the crest of a torrent of fire, flashing the flames of her fury in violent explosions.

The chiefs tried to flee toward the north, but Pele hurled flames beyond them, turning them back. Then they fled toward the south, but again they were forced back upon their own lands. They ran toward the ocean, hoping to escape through the water. But urging the underworld forces to their utmost speed, Pele raced after the chiefs. She shrieked and tore out her hair in handfuls. The floods of lava spread over Kahuku, until the land became desolate from the uplands to the lowlands to the sea.

A canoe lay near the ocean shore. It seemed as though the chiefs had actually found a way to escape, but Pele threw her burning arms around the nearest of her former lovers, and in a moment, his lifeless body was thrown to one side. The lava piled up around his body, and at Pele's command, a new lava wave rose like a fresh crater and swallowed all that remained. The second chief was petrified with horror as Pele seized him in her deadly embrace and called for another outburst of lava. Quickly the Hills of Pele rose out of the lands where the chiefs had ruled. Thus these unfortunate lovers of Pele died and their tombs were created. For many years the Hills of Pele have marked the destruction of Kahuku's lovely land (adapted from Westervelt 1963b).

Even today, just beneath the veneer of modern civilization that covers Hawai'i, the primitive goddess continues to live her passionate existence. Stories about Pele abound, some of these are contemporary adaptations and others are planted firmly in Hawaiian myths and legends. She seems to be a constant presence in the Islands and when one of her volcanoes is erupting, her presence becomes intense, often producing more stories and beliefs about her.

Visitors are easily tempted to pick up pieces of lava rock and take them home as souvenirs of Hawai'i, but each year scores of tourists return those pieces of Pele's lava to the Kilauea Visitor Center on the Big Island. Often the lava rocks are accompanied by letters describing the terrible events that had befallen the tourists and their families, dating from the innocent theft of lava.

Tradition dictates that a menstruating woman should not visit Kīlauea unless she first protects herself with ti leaves on various parts of her body, otherwise she will give offense to the goddess who lives at the volcano. The various kapu must not be broken by intent or by chance.

I felt uneasy when I first gave a public lecture about Pele, so I protected myself by tucking a ti leaf into my blouse. Later I threw a traditional offering into Pele's crater, and now I have reason to believe that I have been given permission to speak about her. At the volcano, as I threw the offering, I prayed to the goddess and asked for her acceptance. The thin, volcanic sulfur steam quickly fanned out and became increasingly thick, until it surrounded me. When it cleared, the offering had disappeared. The ancient kapu are still relevant and are connected to the primitive and elemental power of the goddess.

> E Pele e!
> O Goddess of the burning stones.
> Life for me. Life for you.
> The flowers of fire wave gently.
> Here is your offering . . .
> (Adapted from Westervelt 1963*b*:107)

By some accounts there was a historical Pele who was a chiefess; but as a mythological figure, Pele is a goddess of antiquity. Her mythological position lies deep in our psyches, far below the patriarchal deities who are paramount throughout much of the world and who also reign in Hawai'i. Pele is ancient, and yet for Westerners she provides a startlingly dramatic view of the matriarchal power and consciousness that has been repressed in most societies, along with the mother goddesses who predated the father gods. By whatever name, that repressed elemental energy remains a force with which we must reckon, or, as an unconscious influence, she will rule us from her pit.

Within the last several decades, there has been a shift in the traditional male/female and masculine/feminine definitions and assumptions. Perhaps *shift* is too subtle a word; in some areas the change is more like a revolution. A previously repressed half of humanity, the feminine aspect of life, increasingly is demanding recognition. This feminine quality may be briefly characterized as belonging to the domain of the goddesses, not the exclusive realm of the gods. We can look around and witness a multitude of places where the goddesses, or perhaps the Goddess herself, is re-emerging from centuries of underground entrapment.

Aside from the obvious political and social arenas, the emerging power of the Goddess is manifest in numerous articles, books, commentaries, and arguments that have announced her presence. Jungian psychology, in particular, has attempted to bring the focus of her archetypal meanings to our modern problems and awareness. Each voice that brings additional dimensions to the multifaceted goddess energy, gives us further understanding. We are confronted with a modern development that encourages us to ask how the reality of the goddesses differs from that of the gods.

The mythological Pele is clearly ancient in the family tree of identified goddesses, and she is of special interest because her power remains manifest. The fire goddess is more complicated than simply an expression of elemental destruction. As with the goddess Hina, she combines positive and negative traits in equal proportions. Her violent eruptions are often destructive, but they are also creative, leading ultimately to fertilization of the soil and to additional land. All of the Hawaiian Islands were created by volcanic explosions.

As I write this, I can see the volcanic tuff cone Koko Crater from my window. As always, I delight in the beauty of its raw grandeur. But if, by some astounding quirk of nature, the crater were to stir again to life, many homes, including my own, would be threatened and perhaps destroyed. It is said that Pele is present in any Hawaiian volcano that erupts, and I suspect that several of my neighbors would offer the goddess a bottle of gin, a piece of pork, or some other usual sacrifice.

Among other foods, pork was kapu for women in old Hawai'i, and yet the pig has been a favorite sacrifice to Pele, as well as to masculine gods. The pig has been found almost universally as a symbol of fertility, occurring throughout the world as the sacrificial beast of the fertility goddesses. It is believed that the various pig taboos, such as those of the Jews, Moslems, and early Egyptians, are all related to the sacred nature of the pig as an emblem of the mother goddesses. Interestingly, the only mythological figure who was ever able to tame Pele, even for a while, was the legendary Kamapua'a, the Pig God.

We can only speculate about the relationship between Pele and the sacrificial, often kapu, pig. Pele is a goddess and sometimes she is considered a special deity for women, and yet pork was forbidden to women because it was a body form of a male deity. Although Pele's mythological origins are lost in the mists of unwritten history, there may be a historical connection between the fire goddess and the pig as an ancient symbol of fertility. If so, the pig kapu may be directly related to the matriarchal power of the great goddesses, including Pele, whose mana has been reflected by human females.

The numerous Hawaiian kapu that restricted and separated women were most often related to their menses. Universally menstrual blood has been considered the mysterious magic of creation that is believed to reside in the blood women gave forth in apparent harmony with the moon. Throughout human history, men have regarded this blood with dread, as the life-essence, filled with mana, and completely foreign to male experience (Walker 1983:635). Not only in Hawai'i, but throughout the world, the color red, associated with the fertility and menstrual power of the goddess, has been the most sacred and magical of colors.

Women, of course, are not goddesses, any more than men are gods, but they are handy objects to catch the projection of the goddess image that dwells within us all. Undoubtedly it seemed (or seems) absolutely necessary to place protective kapu between vulnerable human men and the reflected potent, threatening, and bright red goddess power experienced within women. The mana of a goddess such as Pele is immense.

Even as this fiery goddess still moves just below the surface of modern Hawai'i, it is also true that beneath the veneer of our modern manners and mores she continues to live her passionate existence within us. Because I am a woman, and thus intimately aware of the Pele power dwelling at the very core of my own psyche, I try to surround that passion with the protection of taboos. This fiercely primitive female energy, long delegated to the depths of dark pits, erupts constantly from within me and other well-mannered and finely bred ladies. The long repressed and suppressed outrage and rage now exploding from modern women is like another expression of the same volcanic fire. It is raw and potentially dangerous, because it has been lost from the upper world for so long. Let us hope it can be channeled into creative paths before it destroys everything in its way.

Recently I heard a dream that illustrates the dangerous aspects of the explosive Pele reactions. The dreamer is a woman in her mid-thirties with a secure and successful job. She and a man hold equivalent positions and they work under the supervision of the same director, who is a man. Although the woman has spent most of her life defending herself against painful feelings of inadequacy, she is now beginning to appreciate her own strengths as a woman. Lately she has felt increasingly angry because of what she experiences as preferential treatment and more recognition given to the man with the same position as hers. Both he and their director treat her as a "second class citizen," and she is convinced that it is because she is a woman.

> She dreamed that she was in the same room as the two men. Because of the way they had been behaving toward her, she was almost blind with rage. She picked up a graceful ceramic vase and threw it against the wall, breaking it into fragments. (She is proud of this vase because she made it herself.) As she threw it, she screamed at the men in frustration. Then she shouted, "I quit!" and rushed from the room.

The dream certainly reveals the extent of her fury. It can also be seen as a warning that if she does not take responsibility for her hot emotions, she may do something self-destructive. She is in danger of destroying a creative enterprise of her own and also of losing a job that is otherwise rewarding and important to her.

The rage and frustration of modern women is not only understandable, it is appropriate. Nevertheless, the essential element of the anger is archetypal, as well as personal, meaning that there is a fundamental pattern within all women which is stirring. Just as women have been repressed by collective cultural pressures, so, too, is the present feminine eruption a collective experience.

As long as they remain imprisoned in a communal dark dungeon, the vanquished matriarchal powers are unable to evolve into more civilized patterns. A psychological truism is that elements within our basic human nature that are submerged in the underworld remain primitive and uncivilized, steadily gaining enough energy to erupt in various barbaric ways. It is vital that each of us assumes individual responsibility for channeling the outburst of primitive passion into humanizing paths.

The volcano goddess is a personification of a particular aspect of such passionate power, and when experienced collectively, rather than individually, the power remains unrelated to our individual lives. The humanizing of that powerful energy is a task that can be undertaken only by each of us in our unique life situations. Otherwise the nonhuman Woman of the Pit will rule us absolutely from within our own dark craters.

Pele is described as fiery and impetuous as her volcano, and almost as elemental in her passions. It was dangerous to cross her and, as we saw in the fate of the two young chiefs, dangerous to be loved by her. The word *love* is an obvious misnomer. The fire goddess desires, not loves. She passions, not feels. She has no loyalty to any principle but that of her own needs, fires, jealousies, and rages. No wonder I recognize her in myself and in other women; such passion is impossible to ignore, either in its impact or in its consequences. We all possess a Pele aspect rumbling around within us. Rather I should say that we women are under constant threat of being possessed by the Pele within us. When we are possessed by the Woman of the Pit, which is the primitive and elemental female within, we are capable of destroying everything living in our paths.

When such volcanic raw emotion shoots its fire through us, all loyalties to relationships, promises, commitments, and values are forgotten. We swell with awesome power and feel ourselves to be bigger than life, as indeed we are, for we have become identified with an archetypal image, which is a nonhuman, superhuman force. We have lost our human boundaries; we have lost our humanity. The ego, with its ability to remember and choose, has been overwhelmed with divine energy. The very word *pele* means "eruption" or "volcanic spirit." Only after the explosion has spent its blind passion do we look around, witness the destruction, and then as human women we may grieve.

No wonder men tremble before the hot lava flow and instinctively know themselves to be threatened for their very lives, certainly for their manhood. Even when a woman is possessed by the more fertile aspects of the Pele power, a man senses that he is but a pawn, a nameless creature used by the fertility drive of Mother Nature so that the woman may become a mother.

Many of the motionless lava mounds that dot the islands were once female rivals who incurred Pele's wrath. The volcanic expression of the goddess is as destructive to women as it is to men, and we all have good reason to respect and fear it. There is a relevant myth that is told on the island of Hawai'i. It has to do with a flowering shrub called the *naupaka*. There are two varieties of naupaka, one growing near the sea and the other growing in the mountains. Each bears what appears to be split blossoms, five small petals that form half a circle. They look like half a flower. There are several Hawaiian legends about these curious flowers. One story tells of two lovers who were forever separated by the wrath of Pele.

> Pele desired the young man and attempted to lure him away from his sweetheart, the woman who loved him and whom he loved in return. The young man rejected the advances of the fire goddess, thus activating Pele's rage. As was her wont, Pele pursued the young man into the mountains, hurling bolts of fiery lava after him. Pele's sisters, who were more tender and caring than she, took pity on the man and turned him into a flower, thus saving his life. He became the mountain naupaka.
>
> Pele wheeled about and began to pursue the young woman. The goddess chased the woman toward the ocean, but again Pele's sisters intervened and turned the woman into the beach naupaka. And so they exist today, each blooming as half a flower, never to be united again.

For most of us, the fate of the naupaka lovers has been our fate also, but we can change the course of our destinies. We can attempt to develop petals that grow in full bloom, an entire circle. As the naupaka story informs us, we must first become mindful of Pele's power and potential for destruction. My position and judgments about this are complicated; I understand the need for change, and yet I still suffer the problem within myself. I, too, suffer from the degradation of thousands of years of patriarchal oppressions, and my anger is frequently intense. I, too, have a great deal of personal rage and frustration about the long centuries of male domination over women.

At the same time, I can imagine some of the factors that have led to such a fate. The volcanic Pele aspects within me and other women very likely have so terrorized men that they have felt compelled to surround us with taboos or perish. Men have separated themselves from women with restrictive barriers as a means to protect themselves and their masculine virility from annihilation. The authority of the personal mother, which is augmented by the reflected might of the mother goddesses within us all, makes each man's manhood a precious prize for which he has to battle again and again.

Until recently, women have acquiesced to the taboos, perhaps out of their unconscious fear of their own personal and archetypal powers. It may be a compensatory reaction that has led women to become docile daughters of the father world. A necessary step toward growth and awareness requires women to acknowledge the might of a primitive goddess and yet not be blindly ruled by her, either by becoming obedient daughters or devouring mothers.

Such a step is also necessary for men to achieve manhood. The hidden feminine aspects within each man's personality are a powerful influence upon his life. This is especially true if he remains oblivious to his own feminine qualities. It is likely that there is a Pele force within his psychological house, probably hidden from his view as within a covered crater.

Because of the prevailing masculine cultural attitudes, men have repressed the feminine principle within themselves. As a result, their own Pele energy has remained primitive and explosive. Sooner or later, however, Pele will erupt and overwhelm a man's entire personality. When the primitive goddess energy possesses a man, he reacts precisely as though he were the perennial son of a mother goddess, no matter how many compensatory noises he makes with his demands, moods, defenses, sulks, bad jokes, and roaring thunder claps. He is not yet an adult man, with the ability to relate independently to the women in his life or to the world around him.

Today we live in an era in which the repressed feminine elements are rising, and it is urgent that they be differentiated and integrated, by men and women as individuals and by humanity as a whole. It is equally important that these feminine elements become more than characteristics of Pele, Haumea, or any other of the primitive mother goddesses found throughout the world. We women are considerably more complicated than when we function as mothers to our children; the feminine aspects of life embrace more than motherhood.

When the feminine deities and elements were conquered by representatives of the father gods or masculine spirits, they were thrust into the underworld along with the devil, sexual freedom, magic, and respect for the human body and the natural spirit of the earth. Nature herself became hostage. In that underworld place, the feminine spirits remained unconscious. Inasmuch as they were not allowed to develop further, much of the eruptive energy has a revengeful maternal quality. The masculine spirit has violated our world of Nature and she seeks revenge. Fury hath a womanlike or maternal character and we must hasten to civilize her, to offer her our respect and our sacrifices. Nothing new can be created until something of equivalent value is sacrificed to the spirits of creation.

In our society, we are witnessing a re-viewing and re-grouping of old sexual patterns. A rather humorous example of our present confusion is an advertisement that appeared in a Honolulu newspaper. It publicized a "Ladies' Night of the Original World Famous Passion Playboys," performing in an all-male exotic passion dance review. It was limited to the first hundred women aboard a cruise boat, and, in addition to a harbor cruise and the exotic playboys, various kinds of titillating goodies were promised, all for a modest fee. As is obvious in the Pele legends, men can be viewed as sex objects too, as son/lovers, who may be purchased as unfeelingly as the playgirls who are daughter/bunnies.

It appears likely that all of us, men and women alike, can go no further in human development until women become aware of the elements within themselves that have been captive in the underworld. In so doing, they will provide a new experience of the quality called *feminine*. The definitions we have previously given to the term *feminine* are of necessity a reflection of experiences and perception of actual women. And actual women usually have flip-flopped from daughter to mother and back to daughter, always in reaction to prevailing masculine attitudes and needs. Therefore, as we women change, and we must, the very meaning of feminine qualities will shift also. We have a whole treasure still hidden in the underworld.

Some women have so tightly woven the web of protection around their passion that they appear as pale and bloodless shades who wander through this world in a sort of half-life. In response to the unconscious Pele, they fear the power which they unknowingly hold in their pits, although they may dream of volcanoes.

Many years ago, when I felt myself to be completely dominated by men and by the patriarchal culture in which I live, I had a dream that remains the most vivid of my life.

> I'm climbing a mountain, which is dark, as is the sky. Night stretches all around me and there are no stars or moon. I'm about halfway up the mountain and I'm very tired, so I stop to rest and to look up at my destination. On the top crest, I see a huge drum, almost as wide as it is high. Flames leap from the top of the drum, so it's also a volcano. But the drum is also a tremendous candle, because the bright flames are contained by the rim of the drum and pierce the heavy night with a reddish-gold light. Once again I start to climb the mountain.

Because of the emotional impact of the dream, I knew that it had come to me from an archetypal stratum of the psyche. As I was to learn later, it depicted a situation shared by numerous other women. Like others of my conquered sisters, I needed to climb to the summit so that I could experience the power of Pele. I needed to know the hot, burning lava-blood within the core of my own emotional drumbeat. Unfortunately, for quite a while I did a great deal of exploding, thus destroying precious relationships and green growing things lying helpless in my fiery path.

Later I had to travel away from the volcano before I could return in a different way. Now I understand that the dream indicated a way station within my personal myth, which is the story I create of my life as I truly live it.

Previously I had no conscious connection with my own mythologically elemental ground. I was too separated from knowledge of the volcano that is also a drum, like the heartbeat of the earth and of my female reality. I was unconnected with that volcano that is also a candle, with flames to bring light to the darkness. I

had forgotten—as most women have forgotten, if they ever knew
—my power as a woman. This is the power of elemental feminine energy, however defined, which is found in the psychology
of both men and women and is capable of keeping all of us in an
unconscious, immature, and now inappropriate place. Women,
as the visible and manifest human representatives of these qualities, have a special obligation to understand their powers, to
develop them, and to take individual responsibility for them.

Does this sound harsh, directed toward the already over-bur-
dened and oppressed women throughout the world? I see no alternative. Biologically and psychologically it has always been the
feminine, whether as manifested in women or in the anima of a
man, that has given birth to new possibilities for tomorrow. If
indeed we women have within our psychological wombs the
power of Pele, then we have the strong resources available within
ourselves to carry new life to its ultimate delivery.

As long as we, men as well as women, remain in the hidden
clutches of a parental embrace, we are condemned to fulfill only
a portion of our human potential. We remain as mother's sons
and father's daughters, not yet actualized individuals. Like the
naupaka lovers, we are separated from our fuller selves.

> *Mōhala i ka wai ka maka o ka pua.*
> Unfolded by the water are the faces of the flowers.
> (Pukui 1983:237)

9

Kamapua'a, the Pig God

His snout was of great size and with it he dug the earth,
He dug until he raised a great mound,
He raised a hill for his gods,
A hill, a precipice in front,
For the offspring of a pig that was born.

(Beckwith 1951:210)

H<small>E IS</small> racy, rebellious, and outrageous. Imagine a creature, half-man and half-hog, *kupua* (demigod), a ravisher of women, and a destroyer of other demigods and of men. Imagine a rascal, a shape-shifter, who can turn himself into a man or a hog at will, or many pigs, or a pig-shaped fish, or many fish, a tree, or bristly grass like the hair on a pig's back. As a pig, he has an enormous snout, of unmistakably phallic symbolism, with which he roots up rows of earth and prepares the soil for the planting of new seeds.

Kamapua'a, Hog-man, hold still so that I may see you, touch you, and even know you a little. Kamapua'a! Have you no regard for the rules of human society? Have you no shame?

It seems to me that his answering grunt should be understood as an emphatic "No!"

Kamapua'a is one of the most popular figures in Hawaiian mythology, and even today a recitation of some of his adventures brings a smile or a roar of laughter. Just think of the sexual implications of that gigantic snout as it ruts a pathway through moistened earth. It was he who dared to challenge Pele, to follow her lust-smoke to her pit, and, after explosive battles and cosmic upheavals, to rape her. Ah, what a rogue, what a greedy pig. He wants the whole world and tries to devour it.

125

But there is more to him than this. He is also a nature deity who is the rain-making form of the primal god Lono, the akua of fertility and agriculture. Early Hawaiian planters prayed to Kamapua'a, especially the planters of sweet potatoes who considered him an important form of Lono, and vital to the success of their farming. Irregularly shaped sweet potatoes were called "pig's excrement" and belonged to Kamapua'a. His larger droppings formed hills and his snout created valleys. It is even said that his powerful phallus made a groove along the side of a valley on Windward O'ahu that may be seen to this day.

There is so much to him, so many of him, that I hold tightly to my own human limitations. I must not be overwhelmed by his "muchness." He reminds me of my sons when they were of a certain impossible age and of various men I have known all too well. Somewhere he also reminds me of myself.

There are numerous stories about Kamapua'a (*kama*, child or person; *pua'a*, pig or hog). The narration of his adventures is said to have taken sixteen hours, and that is a report from only one of the Hawaiian Islands. Each island has its unique collection of tales about the divine Pua'a, the Pig God. I must not fall into the pig trap of greediness and attempt to discuss them all. I must choose.

Mythological time is eternal; a myth occurs all at once, beginning, middle, and end happen simultaneously and are equal parts of the whole. In a mythological cycle, such as the one starring Kamapua'a, one can start anywhere and will arrive at the same destination as if another beginning had been chosen. The course of the journey depends upon the perspective of the traveler, not the place where the first step is taken. For purposes of clarity, I shall start before Kamapua'a's birth.

The first few lines of a name song that was addressed to his mother follow:

> Be on the watch, be on the watch
> When you give birth, O Hina,
> The eyes of the hog,
> They glance to the heaven,
> And glance to the mountain,
> The son of Hina is a hog with eight eyes
> By Hina art thou . . .
>
> (Elbert 1959:196)

True to prediction, he was born as a hog. His mother, Hina—
yes, one more Hina, or perhaps the same goddess in a different
guise—was understandably distressed at the sight of her pig baby.
Various stories relate how Kamapua'a was rejected by his parents
and quickly adopted by his grandmother. In Hawai'i, children are
frequently raised by their grandparents, but the circumstances
surrounding Kamapua'a's adoption were particularly traumatic.

The grandmother was a sorceress who had brought the family
from Kahiki, the place of origin. She had gone first to Maui, where
her daughter Hina, was born. When Hina was an adult, the sorceress accompanied her daughter to O'ahu, where Hina settled down,
first with one man and then with his brother. Kamapua'a's father
was Hina's second husband. His uncle, 'Olopana, soon developed
into Kamapua'a's first enemy.

Kamapua'a repeatedly stole 'Olopana's chickens, some of which
he gave to his family, thus incurring the animosity of 'Olopana, the
most powerful man in the area. The furious 'Olopana sent guards
to capture Kamapua'a. They caught him in his hog form and tied
him to a pole, intending to take him to their chief. But his grandmother released him with her magic. This happened four times,
and with each release, Kamapua'a killed all of his captors except
one. That man, Makali'i, was permitted to go free and give a report
to 'Olopana.

'Olopana called for all the men in the district to capture his hog-
shaped nephew, who was now cornered in a valley. Kamapua'a
stretched his body up to the top of a mountain, forming a bridge so
that his entire household could escape. (It was here that the phallic
groove was formed.)

After Kamapua'a had followed his household to their new home,
'Olopana consulted a kahuna, and using the kahuna's magic
knowledge he was able to find the fugitive. This time he imprisoned Kamapua'a in a temple, where the hog-man was to be sacrificed. Again Kamapua'a escaped, helped by another kahuna and the
kahuna's sons, and he killed 'Olopana and all of his men, except
Makali'i.

Later Kamapua'a went to Kaua'i, where Makali'i had become
the ruling chief. The hog-man began his more amorous adventures
on Kaua'i and widened the scope of his battles to include other
chiefs and adversaries. He had a confrontation with his parents,
forcing them to acknowledge him as their son. He became a huge
hog who rooted up all the growing crops; he raped, rooted, and battled almost indiscriminately.

Such was his pattern on all the Hawaiian Islands, and even in Kahiki, which he included in his adventurous wanderings. In the legendary Kahiki, he married the daughter (or daughters) of a chief and killed both a rival chief, who was a deity with eight foreheads, and a notorious dog-man, who was also a demigod. As Kamapua'a traveled from one place to another, he left behind seduced, ravished, and abandoned women, as well as myriad dead bodies. His swashbuckling career climaxed at Kīlauea volcano.

He landed in Puna on the island of Hawai'i and proceeded directly to Kīlauea, to the place where Pele and her family lived within the flames. Following the lust-smoke of the goddess, he climbed to a point that was sacred to Pele, and from there he looked down into the pit. The crater of Halema'uma'u, w'thin the restless sea of fire, was kapu, not to be looked upon by outsiders.

The hog-man had assumed the form of a well-built man, for he had decided to engage Pele as his ultimate sexual conquest and had come to woo the goddess. He stood and watched Pele and her sisters, and then he sang a loud chant in their honor. One of the sisters saw him and cried out, "Oh, see that fine-looking man. He stands as straight as a precipice. His face is as bright as the moon. Perhaps if our sister frees him from her kapu, he can be the husband of one of us."

Kamapua'a chanted again, seeking to inflame Pele's well-publicized sexual appetite. He ended with, "Arise. My greetings to you." Pele looked at him with reddened eyes and saw him clearly. She answered from the bottom of the crater, "I would get up if you were a man, but as you are a hog, I will not get up."

Again he chanted. Pele's sisters marveled at the handsome stranger with the flashing eyes and wondered why Pele ignored him. The fire goddess replied that he was not a man, but rather a hog. Her language became stronger, as she ever more graphically described him as a pig.

> Thou art Kamapua'a,
> The buttocks that drop without effort,
> The nose that is pierced by a cord,
> The private that joins the belly,
> The tail that wags behind.
> Answer, Kama, to your name.

By now the hog-man's intentions had shifted from courtship to rape and battle. He said that Pele had sore eyes and then, speaking of a favorite sacrifice to Pele, he chanted:

> Pele is the goddess that eats swine.
> Pele grunts and groans.
> Say, Pele, keep on chiding!
> Say, Pele, keep on chiding!

The taunting, chanted dialogue between Kamapuaʻa and Pele became increasingly hostile. The goddess persisted in scathing descriptions of his piglike characteristics, while Kamapuaʻa's love songs turned to insults wherein he boasted of his power to destroy the entire Pele family of fire deities.

Furiously, Pele ordered members of her family to start a huge fire. When Kamapuaʻa attempted to approach her, she sent her flames over him. Each of them, the fire goddess and the hog-man, stopped screaming only long enough to summon his or her own special deities to aid in the destruction of the other.

Pele ordered her fire-keeper, Lono-makua, to keep up the flames, to burn them ever hotter. The volcano erupted, sending floods of molten rocks into the heavens and covering Kīlauea itself with black smoke. The heat was so intense that people on all the other islands became hot. Kamapuaʻa's whole body was covered with flames.

Naturally, Pele assumed that he was dead, for in a similar manner she had dealt with other suitors and enemies. She ordered the fire to be extinguished, but when she looked again at her sacred hill, Kamapuaʻa stood tall, very much alive. With frustrated rage, the goddess ordered Lono-makua to rekindle the flames.

Then Kamapuaʻa called upon his gods for assistance. Help came in the form of torrents of rain that filled the pit, overflowing it and extinguishing the fire. Only the fire sticks were saved, because Lono-makua had hidden them. The hog forms of Kamapuaʻa descended into the pit, and pigs, more pigs, and still more pigs filled it.

In one account of the stormy battle, Pele chased Kamapuaʻa all the way to the ocean, pursuing him as he changed from one to another of his various body forms. More often it is said that after a long and bitter conflict, Pele was overcome by the strength of her adversary and perhaps by her own sexual cravings. They lay together on a lava field, creating a deep hole in the ground as they mated (adapted from Westervelt 1963b; Elbert 1959; Beckwith 1970).

We do not know who raped whom. Pele had finally met her match, but so had Kamapuaʻa. Perhaps they would have destroyed each other if the fire sticks had not been saved, but those instruments of sexual desire and generation remained a force within the volcano. The fire created by the volcano goddess and the hog-god seems like a reflection of those sticks, rubbing together and igniting into flames as the male fire stick was positioned against the soft hollow of the female fire stick.

Kamapuaʻa and Pele mated in brawlingly impassioned encounters. They loved fiercely and battled noisily, and the earth itself must have trembled with their engagements. Two such passionate figures could not possibly live together for long. After one confrontation too many, Kamapuaʻa assumed the form of a fish and swam off for further adventures. Before he did so, he and Pele divided all of Hawaiʻi's districts between them. Kamapuaʻa took the wet and windward areas of all the islands, while Pele lay claim to the dry districts, those whose lava fields bear evidence of her domination.

By one account, Pele's only child was fathered by the hog-man, and this child became an important Hawaiian ancestor. Depending upon the version of the Kamapuaʻa story, either he drew up another island when he left Pele and settled down to raise a family or he went back to Kahiki, where he had left a wife and child. In one version, his father-in-law in Kahiki ordered castration for the hog-man, thinking thus to keep him from wandering lustfully away. In any case, the high drama of Kamapuaʻa's adventures seems to have diminished after he left the Big Island of Hawaiʻi.

Until then, Kamapuaʻa had behaved as a rogue, often a delightful one, and certainly a seductive one, but his hoglike characteristics were paramount. He was nothing if not swinish; even in his human form, he behaved much like an undisciplined adolescent. He was greedy, egocentric, and chaotic. His numerous sexual adventures are reminiscent of adolescent fantasies and have an undifferentiated quality to them. With the exception of Pele, the women who were his prey were indistinguishable from each other; they were interchangeable victims. He pursued women constantly, some of whom turned into springs of water to escape him, while others became his lovers for a night or two.

During his battle with Pele, her sister Kapo sent her flying vagina off to distant places in order to seduce him away from the battle. At least two imprints remain on the Islands with the configuration of Kapo's seductive vagina. We must assume that the hog-man was both conqueror and prey of any significant vagina that came his way. Like all Don Juans, the conquest was the game, not love, and certainly not commitment. No wonder Pele met her match in him. Both figures operated from the same need for control and power, and both were completely self-indulgent.

Kamapua'a's posture is a statement, "I want!" His actions declare, "I want and will do and will have!" His very animal nature keeps him moving, prowling, searching, lusting, and grabbing. His instincts drive him. They are his own and he lives them to the utmost. He starts as the son of the mother, or grand (great) mother, and remains faithful to her throughout his mythological drama; but he evolves to another phase and continues to evolve throughout the entire mythologem bearing his name.

Historically most deities were originally animals. These gradually evolved into figures, like Kamapua'a, who were half-animal and half-human, thus expressing a transitional stage, not only of the deities, but of the human beings who worshipped them. Later the gods became anthropomorphic and their animal aspects appeared beside them in an attendant role. The animals were then like totem animals, sacred and/or sacrificial.

We can witness part of this evolution in Kamapua'a. In the first part of the cycle, his basic behavior is that of a pig; it is unselfconscious and instinctual. Gradually the emphasis becomes more human, with the piggish periods diminishing. By the time he courts Pele, he has become a man with certain hoglike characteristics. Some of the descriptions of him are of a handsome man whose cape covers the bristles growing along his spine.

We all know men who conceal their piggish nature with sophisticated capes, giving the illusion of untainted humanity. Much the same description might be applied to women of a similar nature, who hide their piggishness with stylish clothes or behind the cover of social masks.

"Piggish nature" is a broad term, suggesting such characteristics as gluttony and lasciviousness. These are human qualities, not those of the actual pig, who behaves in accord with its natural instincts, which are appropriate for pigs. When we speak of the piggish nature of a human being, we are describing certain instinctual drives and behaviors within ourselves that have been projected upon an animal whose behavior we have observed. To one degree or another, we all hide such instinctual drives beneath our more civilized garments. The manner in which we deceive others is of moderate concern here, but the ways in which we fool ourselves may lead to disaster. What is concealed behind the cape of social adaptation are the unconscious instinctual forces that rule our destinies.

We dream of animals as though the psyche itself were holding up a mirror so that we may reconnect with the instinctual foundation of our existence. Animals have always been ready at hand to carry the projections of what lies within us. This was true when the deities were experienced in animal forms and it is true today as witnessed in our dreams. When dealing with the animal images we find in myths and dreams, it is important to keep in mind the divine nature of the beast. There is a deep level of the psyche where instincts have a common root with reflections of the divine, and when we turn our attention to that place an attitude of respect and sacrifice is required. The divine nature of the animal within us has often been thrust into the darkest of pits, and from that unseen place it exerts immense power over our lives.

Dreams wherein an animal is chasing the dreamer, or otherwise behaving in a threatening manner, generally indicate that an instinctual force has been split off from the dreamer's awareness. It has been pushed down into the unconscious, and now it is demanding attention. The more threatening the dream animal, the more the dreamer has repressed that particular aspect of his or her own nature, and the more urgent is the need to integrate it into waking life. Threatening animals are a common motif in dreams, and an entire zoological range of possibilities may be represented. Dogs attack, wolves chase, snakes bite, lions pounce, cats claw, and mythical monsters lurk behind trees. An endless array of animals frequent our dreams, in both threatening and comforting roles, and they can tell us a great deal about the condition of our inner homes. When we are able to relate to animal images in a positive manner, then we can connect with our own instinctual energy and utilize it as a vital life force.

The dreamer's actual experience with an animal determines how the dream image is to be understood. As an example, a person who lives in Florida might dream of a shark that is swimming toward the dreamer, who is frantically trying to flee. The dreamer's associations with the shark might all relate to fearful emotions, because he perceives sharks solely as "killers." On the other hand, a Hawaiian might have a similar dream shark swimming toward her, while she is joyfully swimming to meet it. Even in her dream, she would understand that her 'aumakua is coming to help her, because the shark god is a guardian of her family.

In a similar fashion, the piglike aspects of Kamapuaʻa need to be understood within the context of the Hawaiian culture. Early Hawaiians were keen observers of their environment and must have been aware of the general behavior of pigs, that universally observed in all societies, such as their fertility and habit of rooting in soil. In addition, pigs in Hawaiʻi had a special relationship to the gods and to royalty. As previously discussed, from ancient times the pig was the preferred sacrifice to the gods. Women and little boys were not allowed to eat pork, because of its sacred relationship with the deities. According to various accounts, certain pigs also had the power to recognize royalty and were used to identify living chiefs, as well as to find the buried bones of dead ones. Whether or not pigs actually were able to recognize the scent of royalty, such a legendary ability is used in a number of stories as a deus ex machina.

In general, the pig has been associated with fertility throughout the world and has been a favorite sacrifice to the gods of many people, not only Hawaiians. It has been closely connected with the planting and harvesting of food. As such, the pig has been prominent in various rituals of the mother goddesses, many of whom were originally represented as pigs. Among the American Indians, as among Hawaiians, the pig is understood to be a lunar and thunder animal, and also a rain bearer. The rain-making aspect of Kamapuaʻa is closely associated with the planting and harvesting of sweet potatoes, which was an essential food crop in early Hawaiʻi.

As with all symbols, the pig resists any attempt to define it succinctly. This certainly is the case with Kamapuaʻa, the hog-man who squirms out of reach and escapes with his muchness. *This is your name chant, Kamapuaʻa, make answer!*

If the story of Kamapuaʻa were told as a play, the second act curtain would go down as the hog-man left Pele behind on the island of Hawaiʻi. As is often the case in a good three-act play, the dynamics of the drama are clarified during the third act. At first, Kamapuaʻa was the rebellious adolescent who fought against any father figure who came his way. Then, in the second act, he was the arrogant demigod who, after seducing a multitude of lesser women, dared to confront and engage the goddess of fire herself. He took her on, dealt with her as water does with fire, and when he left her he appears to have been transformed by that fire. The confrontation at the volcano changed him in an important way.

Until then, the emphasis had been on Kamapua'a as a youth. And youth, by its very definition, is a time of transformation and change. He went to the great goddess of the volcano as a youth, but he did not deal with her as if he were a son. He dealt with her as an equal, and it appears that he came out of that encounter with added maturity.

Such a mythological maturation has its echo in human beings. Western culture is moralistic and its ideals are those of adulthood. Not age, with its hoped-for life wisdom, but adulthood, with its relevant worship of responsibility, moderation, commitment, work ethic, and patriotism. The same value seems to have been put on adulthood in early Hawaiian culture. Obviously, the ideals and morals of adulthood were different from those of Western cultures, nevertheless, in each case they stand for the status quo as expressed within that society. This appears to be true in all societies. Even in Western culture, where youthfulness is idolized, the parental establishment rules our lives. Youth implies change, a period of movement and experimentation. Such a phase is threatening to the supporters of the status quo and adulthood because it threatens the very structure of a particular society.

Initiatory rituals carefully guide the pubescent youth along a pathway that will lead him to become a mature adult, as approved by the community into which he was born. (When a Hawaiian boy was taken from his mother and brought into the men's eating house, he was allowed to eat pork.) Seen from the perspective of the adult, the adolescent must change into his opposite: adulthood. From a psychological viewpoint, the adolescent or youthful quality does not evaporate, rather it goes into hiding.

Let us follow Kamapua'a after his affair with Pele, while remembering that within a mythological cycle, all of the scenes are enacted simultaneously. Now Kamapua'a is no longer solely the scamp who "pigged out" with chickens, carnage, and women. Nor is he only the largest hog the world has ever known, the creature who created valleys and large hills, and even a groove or two with his mighty phallus. Now he is one of the body forms of Lono.

I write these words in the winter, during the time of year that is controlled by Lono. Often I am able to witness the god in his rain-making form, for he lives in the dark, full clouds of the winter season. He shows his flashing eyes in lightning, and he makes statements in his thundering voice. He brings winter rain and flooding streams, but he also brings the rainbows that follow the storms. This has been a good year for signs of Lono.

In common with other Hawaiian deities, Lono has many forms or bodies in which he is manifest. These are called *kino lau* (literally, myriad bodies). The essence of Lono is found in hogs, gourds, sweet potatoes, and rain clouds. The most important of these are the heavy rain clouds that periodically blanket the Hawaiian Islands from November through February. These dark clouds are in contrast to the white clouds of tradewind weather, which belong to Kāne. Kāne's color is white, and as previously discussed, he is associated with sunlight. Black is the color of Lono's clouds, and also of the pigs to be sacrificed to him. Lono's black clouds, filled with winter rains, bring needed water to the Islands.

There are numerous Lono names and references throughout the stories and chants about Kamapua'a, including a chant that is credited to his mother, Hina. In it she identifies her son with Lono in several of his body forms.

> Thou are Lonoiki [little Lono],
> Thou are Lononui [great Lono],
> [The desire of] my eyes, my love, O Lono.
> Thou are Hiwahiwa [black, sacred, precious],
> Thou are Hamohamo [the anointed].
> The season of fruit, the heavenly season,
> When the heavens are covered with black clouds.
> (Handy and Handy, with Pukui 1972:340)

Here we have a hog-man who is understood to be an essential aspect of one of the four primary gods of the Hawaiian people, that of the rainmaker. In contrast to the characteristics exhibited by Kamapua'a as he races through the islands, Lono is an upright, solid citizen who is the image of adult maturity and stability. He might be seen as the very spirit of continuity and fruition.

At least fifty Lono gods were worshiped by the early Hawaiians. As the god of fertility, Lono was celebrated in the Makahiki festival of harvest time. Lono-makua (Elder or Father Lono) was the name given to the image that represented Lono at that time; it is also the name of Pele's fire-keeper. Offerings of food and other gifts were given to Lono, as Lono-makua, during the Makahiki festivals, which were held yearly, roughly between October and February. During Makahiki, the high chiefs collected their portions of the annual harvest, before it was made available to the people (Beckwith 1970).

Lono was believed to arrive annually in Hawai'i, when the Pleiades appeared in the eastern sky at sunset. The Makahiki started after the new moon following this sighting. The Pleiades are known as Makali'i to the Hawaiians, which is the same name as the man whose life Kamapua'a spared during the several episodes of mass slaughter. There are numerous references to Makali'i in Hawaiian mythology. He was known as a navigator, an agriculturist, and the holder of the net from which food plants were symbolically dropped during the Makahiki festivals. I have no explanation for Makali'i's position in the Kamapua'a mythologem, but I offer it as one more connecting link between the hog-man and Lono.

There are other links between them. The Makahiki offerings were collected on altars at the borders of the various districts. On those altars, Lono was represented by the head of a hog, which had been carved out of candlenut wood. The candlenut tree is one of the forms of Kamapua'a. The altars were called hog altars, *ahupua'a*, and the land districts themselves were also called ahupua'a.

When prayers to Lono were ritually offered in a temple, an offering of a black pig upon the altar was a requirement. If such a pig was not available, any one of the body forms of Kamapua'a could be used as a substitute.

It is interesting to contrast Lono and Kamapua'a. As one writer observed, in the transmutation of multiple forms, as kino lau, the shapes may change, but the essential elements in them do not (Kanahele 1986:96). Kamapua'a and Lono seem to have similar qualities, the differences are those of degree. As an example, Kamapua'a is greedy, he devours every sweet potato in a field and then starts in on the neighboring fields. Or he kills all of the chief's men (except one), leaving behind devastated battlefields. He does not desire just one woman, or two, he desires every pretty woman who comes his way and several about whom he has only heard.

Lono might be saturnine in his behavior, but he is, after all, a god of fertility, and in one of his forms, a god of lovemaking. He is the god of agriculture and the harvest, and when gifts were collected in his name during the Makahiki festivals, the collection of the contributory gifts was conducted in good taste and according to traditional rules. Although Lono, in effect, outlawed war during the Makahiki, he initiated various traditional games and contests that were played during that time. According to at least one source, Lono initiated those games in honor of his wife, whom he had beaten to death in jealous rage. After this display of passion, Lono's behavior usually was controlled and traditional, thus more adult than that of the irrepressible Kamapua'a. I find it easy to imagine the hog-man as Lono before he became an elder or father, while he was still in his animal or adolescent stage; or, as is more likely, Kamapua'a as expressing the animal/adolescent aspects of Lono, the akua.

This is conjecture; it seems that fluid ideas attach themselves to the pig-god as mud would cling to his snout. I am speaking about these figures, Lono (especially Lono-makua) and Kamapua'a, as psychological forces within ourselves, not as the mythological figures in Hawaiian tradition. As archetypal images, they represent dominants in our personalities, and if we are blind to what dominates us, other people will be pleased to tell us about it.

If a person is identified with the paternal principle, he experiences himself solely as an adult. The paternal dominant rules his personality; the patriarchal voice is authoritarian and absolute, both within and without. The person is judgmental, moderate in habits, saturnine, limited in imagination, and rigid in behavior. He behaves in traditional patterns and expects the same of others. Such conservatism is expressed politically, socially, and certainly in interpersonal relations. Father is in opposition to son or daughter. Father dictates to wife, especially if her personality is sufficiently daughterlike. Father is in control, even when his actual presence is missing. His internalized voice lives on, long after the actual father is dead.

His voice is collective, as well as personal, and has been the dominant one in most cultures for thousands of years. Women, as well as men, are ruled by the paternal principle and they are more victimized by that authoritative voice, because (in a figurative sense) they are never allowed into the men's eating house.

They are not like the little boys who will soon graduate into that valued position. In our culture women are permitted to eat pork, but other taboos are equally isolating. Father may not be greedy, per se, but he demands his sacrifices and he hoards the bounty of the land as his due.

If, on the other hand, the dominant force in a person's character is that of Youth (Kamapua'a being one of the variants), his outer behavior is altogether different. He is passionate, fiery, spirited, imaginative, destructive, rebellious, full of fantasies and wounds both imagined and actual, and is continuously discontented. It has been called a "divine discontent," and it has a divine quality, especially in its more creative moods. The youth moves from one goal to another, one idea to another, from one woman or man to another with mercurial fluidity. Like Kamapua'a and his muchness, he overwhelms us with limitless possibilities.

If Father represents law and order, then Youth represents new potentialities. To further complicate the matter, what we see on the outside as the dominant characteristic represents only half of the situation. If Father is what you see and Youth is what is hidden, the invisible aspect is concealed in the unconscious psyche, both of an individual human being and of an entire society. Then the controlling Father personality finds his own youthful nature projected outside, onto children or anyone else whose temperament does not fit into Father's procrustean bed. Father pitted against son, Father positioned against anyone who activates his fear of whatever is new and untried.

If Youth is what you see and Father is what is hidden, the reverse is true, for individuals and for entire societies. Then rebelliousness is the supreme virtue and it is pitted against law and order, both within and without. Overindulgence results, greediness prevails, whether in the form of substance abuse, sexual promiscuity, or physical violence. It is as though Youth is in revolt against the very limitations set by an internalized Father, and these cause an almost claustrophobic panic.

Absolute freedom versus moderate limits. Muchness versus boundaries. New versus conventional. And adversary against adversary, within as well as without. The split is out there, in the general culture, and it is inside, where the left hand does not know what the right hand is doing. The house is divided against itself.

In time, the rebellious adolescent or youthful spirit may change into his opposite and become a parent in his turn. He becomes identified as an authoritative father figure, and his own adventurous youthfulness is swallowed, becoming unconscious. Then he has a son, or watches the sons of the culture from a pinnacle of propriety, and he finds his own invisible youth projected upon them. The cycle repeats over and over, and the split remains raw and bleeding.

There have been traditional cultures wherein familiar roles are constant and supportive. Fathers are honored by sons who know that one day they, too, will be so honored. Sons are cherished by fathers who see them as heirs to tradition. In such a culture, family units are reflections of the larger units of the community, and because the individual is contained within a stable system, a generational split is rarely exposed—until there is a revolution. Then there is a bloody mess that sweeps individuals into collective carnage that might remind us of Kamapuaʻa's early career.

The split between Parent and Youth occurs in women, as well as in men, although the dynamics are more complicated. Elements of a woman's inner masculine component (animus) battle within her, making it difficult for her to find her own reality. Psychological health requires each of us to heal the split between what we know about ourselves and what has been shoved out of sight. The two sides, which may be experienced as if in opposition, belong closer together. As Pogo wisely observed: We have met the enemy and he is us.

A better relationship between Father and Youth is one example of healing such psychic splits; there are many others. We can find a mythical portrait of such a healing relationship in the Hawaiian image of Lono, when he expresses the qualities of the spirited Kamapuaʻa, who is his rainmaker. Then the hog-man personifies the youthful quality of bringer-of-rain, the fertilizing water from heaven that brings harvest to ever renewing crops. He also personifies the animal energy from which too many of us are isolated in ideas of perfection. Relevant to the healing of such psychic splits is the image of Lono himself, who in one of his many forms is the god of healing.

For me, on a human level, this implies a continuous interaction between two vital aspects of myself. The youthful Kamapuaʻa happens to be very strong in my personality. I set him loose when I started to write about him, but then I had trouble controlling him. He would not stay put behind a fence or restrained by sensible thoughts. He continuously brought in more material, until I was overwhelmed with the chaos.

A man told me a relevant dream he had during a similar situation in his own life.

> He dreamed that an endless supply of little pigs were pushing into his house, so many that they were overflowing the rooms. He could scarcely walk about for fear of stepping on a piglet.
>
> Then he was with an older man, a friend who is extremely patriarchal and judgmental. The friend told the dreamer that "everybody" had been drinking too much wine at a birthday party. (In actuality, there had been no such party.)

When the dreamer and I discussed the dream, we understood the wine to mean "spirits" in celebration of a new birth. As long as he was so split between the Youth and the Father (personified as the older friend), he was unable to set limits to the products of imagination (all those pigs) and could not make the arbitrary choices needed to finish a creative project. Although the dreamer values the "spirits," limits need to be set to the celebration, while not repressing the new birth. The dreamer needed to choose. Such choices are the responsibility of the ego, as the center of consciousness, and evidently his ego had been overwhelmed by the very youthful, creative spirits that invaded his house.

And so, Kamapua'a, we welcome you, but we insist that a balancing force, such as Lono, be with us also. We need to hear what both of you have to say to us. We want to receive all of the ideas and intuitions that you bring in a rainfall of fluid possibilities. All of us need an ongoing relationship with the spontaneous animal spirits, of which you are a divine representative. But we also need assistance from the adult who measures, modifies, and decides just how much is enough, and even brings healing from a divine source. We will try to listen to both of you and then make our choices and suffer them as gracefully as possible. But stay around, please, life would be dull without you.

> O Kama-puaa!
> You are the one with rising bristles.
> O Rooter! O Wallower in ponds!
> O remarkable fish of the sea!
> O youth divine!
>> (Westervelt 1963b:46)

10

Hiʻiaka-in-the-
Bosom-of-Pele

The traveller is ready to go for the loved one.
The husband of the dream.
I stand, I journey while you remain,
O women with bowed heads.
Oh my lehua forest—inland at Kaliu,
The longing traveller journeys many days
For the lover of the sweet dreams.
 For Lohiau ipo.
 (Westervelt 1963b:91)

I HAVE a picture of Pele on the wall of my office. It depicts the awesome fury of the volcano goddess as she destroys a human man who lies at her feet. Another goddess is confronting Pele and her attitude is not one of equal rage, but rather one of compassion and assistance. She is pictured as reaching out her hand to the dying man, trying to pull him from the seething lava. By offering her strength to a powerless human being, she challenges her older sister, who is Pele. The helpful goddess is Hiʻiaka-i-ka-poli-o-Pele (Hiʻiaka-in-the-bosom-of-Pele), and she may have special relevance for us today.

When contemporary Hawaiians speak of Pele's little sister Hiʻiaka-i-ka-poli-o-Pele, they do so in a tone of undiluted love and delight. Many of Pele's other sisters are also named Hiʻiaka, each with a different epithet attached to her name, and they are rarely differentiated from one another in the context of the myths. This one, the youngest Hiʻiaka, was born from the mouth of the earth mother goddess Haumea, who also gave birth to Pele. Pele was born in the shape of flames, while Hiʻiaka was born as an egg that soon transformed into a beautiful girl. She was Pele's favorite sister, and it was she who traveled to Hawai'i tucked in the armpit of the fire goddess.

The best known myth about Pele is one in which this sister is the heroine. The most complete account of the Pele–Hi'iaka legend was translated by N. B. Emerson in 1915. Emerson was one of the most energetic and dedicated of those who translated Hawaiian into English, thus recording the unwritten literature of Hawai'i. In *Pele and Hiiaka: A Myth from Hawaii*, he has woven the translated hula chants into a romantic tale of love, passion, jealousy, and high adventure.

A large number of the traditional hula chants and dances performed today celebrate some aspect of the myth about Pele and Hi'iaka. Hi'iaka's journey across the archipelago of Hawai'i is the thematic thread holding the dances and chants together in what is hula's most important mythological story. Here are the bare bones of a lengthy poetic drama:

> Long ago Pele and her many sisters traveled from their volcano home to the seashore. There, beside the waves at Puna, Hi'iaka-i-ka-poli-o-Pele (hereafter referred to as Hi'iaka), sang for Pele, giving us the earliest recorded description of the hula.

> > The voice of Puna's sea resounds
> > Through the echoing hala groves;
> > The lehua trees cast their bloom.
> > Look at the dancing girl Hopoe;
> > Her graceful hips swing to and fro,
> > A-dance on the beach Nana-huki:
> > A dance that is full of delight,
> > Down by the sea Nana-huki.
> > (Emerson 1978:2)

Hi'iaka then hurried to her lehua groves. There she gathered flowers, wove them into leis, and danced with her dearest friend Hōpoe. It was Hōpoe who had taught Hi'iaka the hula arts of dance and song.

Meanwhile Pele went into a cavern and fell into a deep sleep. While asleep, Pele heard the sound of a faraway hula drum, and her spirit-body rose up from her physical body as she followed the sound across the ocean to the island of Kaua'i. The drumbeat led her to the house of Lohi'au, the uncommonly handsome chief of Kaua'i. She went to his hula hall, where people had gathered to celebrate. There Pele assumed the form of a beautiful young woman and, entering the hall, she walked straight to Lohiʻau.

Soon Lohiʻau took Pele to his private quarters and there they stayed for three nights and three days. Then Pele left, promising to send for him. He tried to keep her in his human embrace, but she rose in her spirit-body and floated away. Grief stricken, Lohiʻau hanged himself with his loincloth.

Back in Puna, Pele's sisters grew anxious about her long sleep. They sent for Hiʻiaka, who was the only one allowed to awaken Pele. Young Hiʻiaka had the beauty of an opening blossom, with deep feelings that reached out like a bridge to all that surrounded her. Moreover, she was gifted with quick intuition and an inner vision with which she could see future events. She was unswerving in her devotion to Pele.

After Hiʻiaka had awakened Pele and they returned to the volcano, Pele asked each of her sisters to go to Kauaʻi and bring back Lohiʻau. None of the older sisters would do this; each fully understood how dangerous such a mission would be. Only the youngest Hiʻiaka agreed to go.

Before she left the volcano, Hiʻiaka extracted a promise from Pele that she would not touch Hiʻiaka's lehua groves or harm her friend Hōpoe. Hiʻiaka asked for, and received, some of Pele's mana to protect her on the journey. Then Pele warned her sister not to touch Lohiʻau and to return with him within forty days.

Shortly after she left the volcano, Hiʻiaka found female traveling companions, only one of whom traveled with her all the way. Her journey was as perilous as had been feared. The Islands were inhabited then with thousands of evil spirits, including the most dangerous *moʻo* (monsters). There was a moʻo in the form of fog and sharp rain that tried to bar her path, but Hiʻiaka entangled it and its followers in fast-growing vines. More moʻo appeared, and numerous other traps awaited her, but Hiʻiaka's powerful mana enabled her to detect the entrapments and to turn them back upon the evil sources.

There were ocean channels to cross and ridges to climb. On Oʻahu, her most famous battle occurred when she crushed the moʻo Mokoliʻi. Today we still can see its tail in the ocean, now in the form of an islet. If Hiʻiaka thought of Lohiʻau at all, it is likely that he seemed only an object of Pele's desire and a gift to bring back to her sister. Her battles occupied most of her attention. By the time she reached the chief's home, she had cleared the Islands of the worst of the evil spirits and had made the land safer for the people.

When Hiʻiaka arrived near the home of Lohiʻau, she discovered

that he was dead. Soon she was able to perceive his ghost body and to catch it. Taking the ghostly form back to the chief's dead body, she began to force his spirit back into his flesh. After ten days of chanted prayers, she succeeded in bringing Lohiʻau back to life and full health. During those ten days, the people of the area followed Hiʻiaka's command and continuously danced hula.

When Hiʻiaka, Lohiʻau, and her companion began their return trip, the forty days allowed by Pele had passed. Most of Hiʻiaka's chants during the homeward journey have a recurrent refrain of sorrow, for by now she had a vision of Pele's treachery. She saw in the heavens that Pele had become consumed with jealousy and was convinced that her little sister and Lohiʻau would become lovers. The enraged Pele had sent her hot lava to destroy the lehua groves, and Hiʻiaka's friend Hōpoe had perished with them.

Hiʻiaka suffered terrible conflict. She tried not to believe the destruction that her vision revealed, but Pele's broken promise filled her with grief. To add to her anguish, she and Lohiʻau were increasingly attracted to each other.

At one point in their travels, near what is now called Honolulu Harbor, they spent the night with a seeress named Pele-ʻula, who was a former lover of Lohiʻau's. The two women played the popular game kilu, with Lohiʻau as the prize for the victorious contestant. Although Hiʻiaka won possession of the man, and he turned to her eagerly, she remained true to her promise and refused to touch him.

At last they reached the volcano. There Hiʻiaka found that her vision had been true. Black desolation and ruin covered the formerly lush land, and Hōpoe had been turned to lava rock. Full of anguish, Hiʻiaka led Lohiʻau to the edge of the crater and made love to him within full view of Pele. The enraged fire goddess encircled the lovers with her flames. Hiʻiaka was protected by her mana, but Lohiʻau was devoured by hot lava and died a second time.

After more adventures Lohiʻau's spirit was found and once more restored to his body. There are several versions of the myth's ending, but in all of them, Hiʻiaka and Lohiʻau were at last reunited (adapted from Beckwith 1970; Emerson 1978).

The hula chants in the Pele–Hiʻiaka myth, which are enchanting even in translation, record the travels of the young goddess. Frequently the words have at least a double meaning, as when the accounts of weather and landscape also portray the emotions of the speaker. As is often the case with Hawaiian chants, a description of natural surroundings then implies an expression of inner geography as well.

> Vile, vile is this Koolau weather:
> One soaks in the rain till he's full.
> The rain, it pours . . .
> Heavy and sad, alas, am I,
> Mine eyes, a bundle of tears,
> Are full to o'erflowing.
> (Emerson 1978:90)

What Hiʻiaka's journey thus portrays is a remarkable blend of inner and outer realities, and it is meant to be understood in such multiplicity. Hawaiians are alert for the hidden kaona within the apparent shell of factual statement, and it gives them added delight when there are layers to unfold. Hiʻiaka's journey describes the incredible beauty of the Hawaiian Islands, but it also speaks of a goddess' odyssey from innocent youngest sister to an important figure in her own right—goddess and yet woman, fulfilled by feminine experiences.

Hawaiian mythology is alive with a multitude of gods, goddesses, and other deities, and yet Hiʻiaka-i-ka-poli-o-Pele has captured the hearts of Hawaiians in a manner unlike that of any other figure. She delights me also, and I continue to explore the reasons for her appeal.

> Hiiaka, thou thatcher of towns,
> Hiiaka, soul of the flame-bud;
> Hiiaka, emblemed in ti-bud;
> Hiiaka, who dwells on the headland;
> Hiiaka, who parts heaven's curtains;
> Hiiaka—of Pele's own heart!
> (Emerson 1978:225)

Aside from her importance in the traditions of hula, Hiʻiaka is considered both a sorceress and a healer. The powers that Pele had given her enabled Hiʻiaka to vanquish, by means of sorcery, those whom she perceived as her enemies. Emerson's translation of the myth is highly romantic and rather sentimental. He makes light of what must have been heavy sorceress' magic, although he does include an episode wherein Hiʻiaka dashes the soul of a man against the rocks because of his lack of hospitality toward her. There are writers who describe Hiʻiaka as a deity of dark sorcery. Inasmuch as mana, like psychic power, is neither positive nor negative, neither good nor evil, but is supernatural power

directed by the sender, a certain ambiguity always exists between
healing and sorcery.

Be that as it may, Hiʻiaka is most often portrayed as a healer,
having brought both Lohiʻau and another man back to life during
her journey across the Hawaiian Islands. Frequently she is
invoked in healing prayers, either alone or in conjunction with
another deity of healing. In addition she is considered to be the
guardian of womanly rites, and, inasmuch as such rites universally include fertility magic, Hiʻiaka's mana has a strongly feminine quality. Goddess, so worthy of homage, she is also a woman
and may be followed as a guide. Speaking to her women companions, she said:

> Be you two stubborn as men!
> Let me be guideful as woman.
> (Emerson 1978:48)

Although the myth portrays Hiʻiaka with many of the powers
and aspects that characterize a deity, there is a human quality to
her with which we can identify. She is a heroine but does not project the larger-than-life aura of Pele. There is a vulnerability
about Hiʻiaka, a tender sensitivity, a sense of commitment and
conflict, sadness, gaiety, or despair. Her emotions do not have
the same raw primitive quality that characterize those of Pele,
nor those of most other Hawaiian gods and goddesses. To put this
thought into psychological terms: Pele is solely an archetypal figure, and as such she represents an elemental force to be found in
numerous other mythological images. Hiʻiaka, however, possesses individual qualities that are unique.

I find it interesting that Hiʻiaka's journey from the volcano to
Kauaʻi is in the opposite direction from Pele's journey when she
originally searched for her home. This directional reversal finds
its echo in another kind of change. The story of Hiʻiaka's odyssey
speaks of a time in human development when the basic Pele
image was becoming differentiated, moving toward a different
experience of the feminine principle, however that principle is
defined. As Pele's youngest sister, Hiʻiaka symbolizes a younger,
thus newer, aspect of the fire goddess herself. The other sisters
who were born before the heroine, represent transitional stages
of development, culminating in the birth of the new goddess as

an egg. Throughout the world's mythology, the figure who is hatched from an egg has special, often miraculous, significance.

To simplify what is a complicated idea, Hiʻiaka-in-the-bosom-of-Pele brings a new development of the feminine experience, both within women and men, one that relates to the heart. The epithet *poli* in her name means "bosom" and poetically signifies the heart. Although she is a deity, she seems at least partially human, and she is capable of love. She loves Pele and all members of the Pele family. She loves her friend Hōpoe, and she loves and protects her traveling companions. Her very loyalty to Pele and her growing love for Lohiʻau provide the conflict that changes an innocent girl into a mature and wise woman-goddess.

Too often, conflict is regarded as a negative experience, a stressful state of affairs to be avoided completely or dulled in whatever manner is possible, including the cultivation of happy thoughts. Nevertheless, it is a psychological fact that no growth or development is possible without the pain of conflict that is suffered consciously and courageously. Without the painful feeling of being pulled apart by two equally strong emotions or choices, most of us would remain rooted in one spot, that of our familiar ground.

Rarely are human conflicts as melodramatic as those of Hiʻiaka, but they are filled similarly with tension and suffering. Does a man stay with his ailing mother or his independent sweetheart? Does he choose his wife or the woman with whom he is having an affair? Which career will be followed when both are of equal attraction? Does a woman choose one man or another? Or neither? Does she decide to have a child or seek to better her professional position? What does she do when she and her husband each needs to live in a different city because of the demands of their individual jobs? Which? Who? How? Only the struggle with conflict between equally valued choices leads us to cross over to another, as yet unknown, territory.

It is clear that some kind of bridge is necessary in order to make a safe crossing from the known position or ground to an unknown place. I am struck by an interesting episode in the Hawaiian myth. When a moʻo monster made a false bridge of its tongue to lure Hiʻiaka and her companions to destruction, Hiʻiaka saved herself and the others by using her *pāʻū* (a kind of skirt) as a bridge. Her magic pāʻū conquered other difficulties also.

The pā'ū, as an expression of a certain feminine attitude, does more than cover Hi'iaka's sexual parts, it also expresses an aspect of her femininity that enables her to move safely into the future. This particular feminine perspective, whether found in a woman or in the anima of a man, miraculously bridges the gap between an old stance and whatever lies on the other side of the abyss. A bridge constructed of the tongue of a mo'o, however, is a regressive, faulty attitude that collapses when the weight of reality steps upon it.

The word *mo'o* is defined as a lizard, reptile of any kind, dragon, serpent, or water spirit. There are the actual mo'o that I see every day. They are the small lizards or geckos that scurry along the walls and ceilings in Hawaiian homes and obligingly catch and eat insects. On a grander scale, there are the mythological mo'o, which are similar only in name and shape.

The mythic mo'o are a major classification of 'aumākua, the ancestral guardian gods, and these are generally revered. When they are not the 'aumākua for a particular family, however, mo'o are often perceived as the enemy of human beings, or, at the very least, as spirits to be dealt with cautiously. The behavior of the mo'o in the Hi'iaka myth seems to indicate that these are not the 'aumākua of any family, but that they are dangerous spirits to be controlled or overpowered. It has been suggested that the mo'o spirits were ancient and powerful gods of the Hawaiian people who were conquered by later, anthropomorphic deities. Hi'iaka's battle with the mo'o might be illustrative of such conquests.

It appears that the Polynesians brought the worship of mo'o with them when they spread across the Pacific to colonize the islands. The lizard gods, or monsters, are known by several names, including moko or mo'o, elsewhere in Polynesia, but the mythological resemblance is clear. In New Zealand, for example, even small and innocuous lizards have been regarded with inordinate fear by the Maori. Perhaps the fear and/or awe felt toward these often harmless reptiles results from earlier experiences with crocodiles when the Polynesians lived in Melanesia or other regions farther to the west.

Whatever may be the historical origin of the mo'o as a reptilian monster or god, within the context of this myth I think we can best understand the primeval mo'o as dangerous dragons. As archetypal images, dragons are frequent figures everywhere. Because dragons are a collective image, belonging to numerous cultures, it is not surprising to find them, as mo'o, in Hawai'i also. Whether Hi'iaka's battles with them should be interpreted as religious victories, wherein a more advanced religion replaced an older one, or as an indication of psychological development is a moot question. It is likely that the change was both religious and psychological, because both perspectives involve the human psyche, or soul.

Myths and legends that contain dragon battles are found all over the world. Mythologically the hero's battle with a dragon is a common theme, usually portraying conquest over a feared communal enemy. The dragon has imprisoned the maiden or maidens, is devouring the population, or is guarding the treasure. In each case, a victory over the dragon brings a positive new condition. Similar to the snake, its mythical first cousin, the symbolism of the dragon includes that of transformation.

Psychologically a battle with a dragon may portray the human ego, usually as a masculine hero, fighting against his own regressive tendencies and by extension against those of the society to which he belongs. Often the monster seems to symbolize the destructive and devouring aspects of the Great Mother, she who would keep us trapped in mushy swampland. Such a dragon, in whatever shape it is found, would try to pull us back and down into its regressive Queendom. All three of these explanations of the conquest of mo'o, religious, mythological, and psychological, have parallel themes. In Hawai'i, as long as the feminine principle was dominated by Pele in her primitive and inhuman aspects, it follows that the Islands would be covered with the swamplike instincts of the mo'o.

In a man's psychology, the dragonlike quality of the feminine principle ties him to the archetypal Great Mother, about whose power in his life he is unaware. As discussed in the chapter about Pele, she possesses him from a hidden place, keeping him forever a son-lover who is unable to relate as adult to adult, either to the women in his outer life or to the feminine elements within himself. In a woman's psychology, insofar as she is caught in the dragon swamp, she is unable to develop her reality as an autonomous human being. She has not yet found her own ground upon which to stand.

In most Western myths, the hero is male and he fights to separate himself from symbolic containment in the Great Mother womb, as well as from dependency upon his personal mother. As his further development demands that he become free of her, the nourishing qualities of the maternal source become dragonlike and devouring. The positive mother turns into a negative one. At this point, the battling hero fights his own need to be taken care of in every way and to receive unqualified love no matter what he does.

Battle with the dragon is necessary before the hero can continue his journey. In no other manner can he claim his own individual manhood, with energy available to make individual choices and summon the will power to set goals and achieve them. The treasure that the dragon is guarding is thus the man's own individuality. This heroic masculine model has been the mythological theme in numerous cultures since the beginning of the patriarchal era. It is a myth as dreamed by patriarchal societies and it expresses a needed evolution in human history, as well as a needed development in a man's personal history. Historically and psychologically the myth's relevance for women has been less clear, because women, as human reflections of an archetypal image, have been conquered along with the dragons.

Pele and Hiʻiaka take us further back in mythological time, when the powers of the matriarchy were still apparent. It was a time when people felt themselves to be an integral part of the universe, participating both consciously and unconsciously with everything and All. Thinking tended to be magical, and it was with magic that humans sought to control their fates. Hiʻiaka used magical means to do battle with the moʻo dragons, and it was with these powers, not physical strength, that she was victorious. Her methods were those of the feminine world, even though a primitive one, which continues to exist whether or not it is perceived.

In this sense, Hiʻiaka can be seen as a new feminine spirit, still relevant today, who battles against the dragon instincts and prevails. Yet she remains loyal to her own basic roots, dramatized as her older sister. Hiʻiaka remains a member of the Pele family of fire deities, indeed she has no choice. But within her character, the fiery qualities of passion and fertility have evolved into a form more suitable for human integration. She personifies the positive symbolism of fire, including that of transformation.

Many women are still in the same psychological situation as Hiʻiaka, so her journey remains pertinent. Before we can proceed, we must reestablish our connection with our own fiery roots, because we certainly cannot transform what we are unaware of possessing. Similarly, many women are unaware of the magical quality of their thinking and the lack of discriminating focus in their dealings with the world. What is said about women is equally applicable to the feminine aspects of men. When a man overindulges in magical, wishful thinking and has difficulty focusing on his life's goals, he seems to be a victim of the negative feminine parts of his own personality.

Hiʻiaka's heroism was thrust upon her because the old ways were no longer appropriate. Daily I see such heroism exhibited by modern women, who are making valiant efforts to free themselves from previously swamplike or volcanic ways to be women. Their efforts are heroic, and in each case, they are filled with enormous conflict and battle, as well as the obvious rewards. Such heroism seems necessary and it is part of the collective spirit of our time. Some of us, however, get stuck in a heroic posture and then we begin to suffer various physical and psychological symptoms. A certain amount of heroic posturing seems inevitable, but it is important that women not remain fixed, either in the heroic stance or in the symptoms. We need to move on, to continue our journeys to a more integrated goal, mythologically expressed as Hiʻiaka's union with Lohiʻau.

The evolution of the feminine principle, as personified by Hiʻiaka, was a necessary step at a particular point in human history. It is not to be duplicated in form now. Each of us will have to distinguish our own moʻo for battle and our own resolution to conflicts and loyalties. The old models seem increasingly irrelevant to our modern lives, which are often filled with unforeseen dilemmas.

As an example, Linda is thirty-five years old and has reached the place professionally where early promise is beginning to bring satisfying rewards. Although her work requires long hours and constant attention, she uses the word *love* when she describes her feelings about it. She loves her work. Nevertheless, she and her boyfriend, with whom she has lived for two years, would like to get married so that they can start a family. The relationship is a good one, and she and the man love each other deeply. Linda would also "love" to have children and she feels strongly that she would need to give them a great deal of her time and energy while they were young.

Despite her heroic plans to do everything and do all of it well, something will have to change or Linda will begin to falter. Her boyfriend is putting pressure on her, as is her own biological clock. The pressures upon her are those of love, but the conflict is painful. She has not yet found a way to do justice to her career, her hoped-for children, and her relationship with her boyfriend. Choices will require her to sacrifice some part of her desires, at least temporarily. Linda's dilemma is a modern problem and one that she must resolve as quickly as possible. Sacrifice of some sort will be necessary, which is always the case when we reach a crossroads and there must be roads not taken.

Until recently, few men or women had so many alternative roads to travel or as many choices to make. The signposts were clear and even if they led to a boring, exhausting, or inappropriate life for any particular person, the paths were there to be followed or severe penalties were exacted. All women obeyed certain conventions or they were considered to be unnatural, and then they were ridiculed and often isolated. The same was true for men, although their rules were somewhat more flexible, at least for those who had the economic freedom to pursue the work of their choice. Human beings were expected to behave in certain preordained masculine or feminine ways and there was little room for maneuver. The inarticulated assumption was: thus it has always been, will always be, and must be now and forever. (A silent "amen" was usually added.)

As an example of such a condition, we need go no further than to Linda's parents. Linda's father took over his own father's business and developed it from a small grocery store to a large, privately owned supermarket. He is anxious to retire and finally begin to "enjoy his life." Linda's mother, like her own mother before her, is a homemaker whose days are filled with the concerns of her husband and children. She is waiting eagerly for Linda to get married, settle down, and have her own children. There has been a certain void in Linda's mother's life and she hopes that grandchildren will fill it.

Thus far, the mother has been contained in a conventional role, which has brought few major conflicts. This would change quickly, however, if her husband dies before she does, or if he decides to leave her for the younger woman with whom he has been having a secret affair. Such a crisis might propel her out of conventional responses, and into unplanned distress and conflict. If she is fortunate, it will ultimately lead to a more meaningful life.

It is appropriate that Pele, as the primitive archetypal mother goddess, and therefore completely unconscious, pushed Hiʻiaka out of the family nest, hot as it might be, and into her own journey, which included love. Hiʻiaka's journey can be seen as an uncharted sequence of steps, each step requiring an immediate response. She changed as a result of meeting unplanned experiences and problems and transformed herself with her changing attitudes.

Although Hiʻiaka loved Lohiʻau, she sacrificed sexual union with him during the journey. She differentiated sexuality from feelings, a subtlety of response that was impossible for Pele. Hiʻiaka was tempted, but even when she won sexual possession of the man in her kilu game with Pele-ʻula (red-Pele), she remained faithful to her promise. Pele-ʻula probably should be understood as an emotional fiery-red and passionate aspect of Pele herself, one who had been in relationship with Lohiʻau previously and set yet another test for Hiʻiaka. Each trial tempered Hiʻiaka's character to a more refined shape and each choice brought additional strength. I have yet to discover an easier route to transformation than one which contains such trials.

As discussed previously, when we acknowledge the Pele power within our own psyches, then we can experience it as the power of a goddess, not ours. And as we separate ourselves from that archetypal energy, we can begin to become ourselves. Then the energy becomes available for our tasks as human beings.

Although she is a goddess, Hiʻiaka presents us with certain aspects of such a separation. She, the youngest sister of raw, elemental passion, manifests the principle of human love, a value which points her way toward increased autonomy. The path she follows is an individual one and the steps she takes are her own. Here, also, we can only utilize the qualities of the young goddess if we are not identified with her, but rather we recognize what she represents within ourselves. To be identified with the principle of "love" is as unconscious an attitude as any other such identification, including that of motherhood.

The same may be said of Lohiʻau. Understanding him as a certain representation of a woman's masculine component, we can realize how crucial it is that we, as women, redeem our own masculine or yang energies from the immobilizing force of the mother image. It is during the attempt at such redemption that some women take on the heroic stance that is difficult to shift. Heroism is necessary, but as a tool to be used for life's purposes, not as a cloak which would envelope the entire personality.

In the myth, Lohiʻau is hardly a hero. Very little of the heroic is evident in his actions, unless we consider that marathon honeymoon with Pele as sexual heroism. Actually, Lohiʻau is an anti-hero, and I assume that his lack of heroism is because of the power of the volcanic goddess who rules his psychology and renders him rather limp. As a chief, he is the carrier of the cultural heritage of his people, and thus he represents the collective spirit of his time and place. Until Hiʻiaka's journey, his land was filled with the dragonlike moʻo, so the atmosphere might have been rather threatening.

A Lohiʻau type of man is a creature of the mother. She, whether found in an outside woman or in his own anima, drives him, controls him, gobbles him up, and then spits him out when she is sated. Rarely does he have enough energy to revolt and follow his rebellion to resolution. When he is frustrated, he often responds with passive aggression, depicted in the myth as Lohiʻau's suicide.

In a woman's psychology, the inner anti-hero keeps her from channeling her creative energies in positive human directions. The masculine principle, which she needs in order to set a goal and work to achieve it, fails her at each way station. It is as though she picks up her pen to write and it collapses in her hand or runs out of ink. She pulls her bow to shoot an arrow at a stated target and the arrow turns into a wet noodle, while she, in generalized frustration, may explode in fiery rage or dissolve in a puddle of mush.

Handsome though he may be, Lohiʻau remains a mama's boy throughout the myth. It is a sticky stage, dramatized with moods and sulks, and a man can remain stuck in it throughout his life. He grows older and becomes increasingly like a vegetable, his passivity transfers him from puberty to senility with barely a ripple.

Lohiʻau died twice because of Pele's passions. I suspect that if Pele's power had remained absolute, without the humanizing influence of Hiʻiaka, he would have stayed dead the first time, only to be replaced by another victim who would meet a similar fate. Alternatively, he might have died endlessly, season after season, forever sacrificed to the fluctuating passions or rhythmical fertility demands of the primitive goddess. As it is, Lohiʻau's two deaths and two rebirths can be viewed as transformations.

My own belief is that while Hiʻiaka worked over the awakening body of the chief, slowly bringing him back to life, she was struck by the beauty of his manhood. It would follow that they were both somehow transformed by the days and nights of gradual awakening; while she was becoming sexually adult, he was being prepared to awaken to a new life and a new love. Such is the power of feminine healing.

We know little about what happened to Lohiʻau after his second death and rebirth, but evidently he acquired qualities that prompted Hiʻiaka to leave the volcano and live in harmony with him for the rest of his life. She remained a goddess, but also became a woman. Presumably Lohiʻau became less limp and more able to be a man to Hiʻiaka after his second resurrection.

A guide such as Hiʻiaka personifies feminine qualities that serve human life, both for men and women. She has the warmth and light of a transformed fire deity and can gift us with the ability to truly live our lives.

When I, as a woman, am loyal to my basic nature, raw and primitive as it may be, and yet differentiate myself from it by separating from the volcano and embarking on my own journey, I may be able to touch the Hiʻiaka quality within myself. When I learn not to divide my loyalties and loves, but to suffer the conflicts they are sure to bring, gradually I may discover what belongs to me.

During the course of Hiʻiaka's long and perilous journey, she found, in the here-and-now of actual experience, what belonged to her own reality, not to that of her older sister, whose domain is archetypal, not individual. Hiʻiaka discovered her own powers during her various encounters and defined her own boundaries as she did so. In human terms, this is a healing journey because it brings previously undiscovered parts of our personalities together in a new way. It is a movement toward wholeness, a process which Jung has termed *individuation*.

No healing is possible without the inner, living waters of the soul, which are always feminine in quality. In the picture on my wall, Hiʻiaka is depicted as reaching out with the hand of love to the dying man at her feet. She is dressed in her pāʻū, which tradition describes as made of *palaʻā*, a lace fern used for healing. The scene portrays a possibility within us all. Humanity, as we know it today, is suffering a terrible destruction of spirit and is in danger of total fragmentation and annihilation.

All of us, men and women alike, have urgent need of the healing, life-giving power of the Feminine, which is the might of feminine energy channeled into creative paths. It is hoped that path will lead us to the place where the Feminine and Masculine join and conceive new life.

Hiʻiaka brought healing and life. Sometimes she is called Hiʻiaka-i-ka-wai-ola (Hiʻiaka-in-the-water-of-life). When she healed Lohiʻau in the dark cave of death, she sprinkled him with water from her calabash, repeatedly calling upon the gods as she chanted. And while the people danced hula, thus channeling mana from the gods, Hiʻiaka brought their chief back to his rebirth.

> I make you grow, O Kane!
> Hiiaka is the prophet.
> This work is hers.
> She makes the growth.
> Here is the water of life.
> *E ala e!* Awake! Arise!
> Let life return.
> The taboo (of death) is over.
> It is lifted.
> It has flown away—*Amama* [The prayer is done].
> (Westervelt 1963*b*:115)

11

The Red Feather

Truth flew on the wings of time
and I knew it not.
I heard the song when a bird
brushed my face.

I<small>T IS</small> the most treasured gift I have ever received from whatever
spirits accompany me when I walk on the beach. I found it just a
few days after moving to Hawai'i. A small red feather protruded
out from the damp sand. Its bright tip was free and gently stirred
in the soft tradewinds. After I brushed off the sand clinging to its
velvety fringes, I cradled the feather in my palm and realized that
it was a portent. A message from somewhere about something.

The red feather became my passport in a new land. Perhaps it
would be more accurate to say, in the way of fairy tales, that I followed the feather's imagined lead when the winds of fancy blew
it in unexpected directions. During the ensuing years I have kept
it safe, knowing that it came to me from the other side, from the
mythological plane of existence. This is true for me, whether or
not it is factual, because the feather seems like a visible souvenir
of vertical adventures.

Bird feathers were the most valued possessions of the ancient
Hawaiians, and red feathers were associated with royalty and the
deities themselves. Not only in Hawai'i, but universally, birds
symbolize transcendence, the vertical movement between earth
and heaven, between human beings and the gods. Feathers usually partake of the same spiritual quality as the birds themselves.
To create feathered gods, as was done by early Hawaiians, or to
wear feathered cloaks, as was permitted only to the chiefs, are
statements of the same symbolic reality. Feathers bring the mana

of the birdlike deities and connect us with transcendent and instinctual knowledge, with the magical power of the symbolic bird (Cooper 1978).

There is a story told by those who recall ancient Hawaiian myths:

> When the demigod Māui was young, the people of Hawai'i could not see birds. The invisible birds flew around houses and the flutter of their wings was heard, as were the stirrings of branches and leaves when the birds alighted. Then there would be music, and the people would stop whatever they were doing so that they could listen to the sweet sounds. They thought the music was made by gods who were unseen by mortals.
>
> Only Māui could see the birds; he had vision as clear as the dawn. He rejoiced in their varied forms and brilliant colors, and when he called to them they would come to rest upon the branches above his head. They sang their happiest songs for him.
>
> One day a visitor came to Hawai'i from another land. The visitor boasted of the many wondrous things in his own country, making the Hawaiians feel that they had nothing fine enough to boast about. But Māui was never one to refuse a challenge, so he called to the birds. They came to him from all the islands, and the songs they sang flew on every side.
>
> After the visitor was impressed by the mysterious music, Māui decided to remove the veil between the people and the birds. He wanted everyone to honor his flying friends. So he chanted magic words, and suddenly the Hawaiians, as well as the visitor, could see the birds revealed in their glorious tropical plumage.
>
> The beautiful red birds, the scarlet i'iwi and the crimson 'apapane, and the birds with their precious patches of yellow feathers, the 'ō'ō and the mamo, were a joy to both eye and ear—as were all the other birds that flew throughout Hawai'i. Forever after they occupied important places in Hawaiian myths and traditions, sharing their beauty as well as their songs with the people (adapted from Colum 1973).

Perhaps Māui did more than remove a veil between the Hawaiians and the birds that inhabit the natural landscape of Hawai'i. He may have made it possible for the people to perceive the feathered spirits that dwell in the mythical realm. These are the birdlike spirits that fly with wings on wind, bringing messages for those of us with eyes to see and ears to hear and hearts to receive the melodies. But for many people, the veil remains, as

though Māui had never removed it. Life on the other side, within the mythical realm, remains invisible and often threatening. Such people seek riches solely in the manifest world and wonder why they continue to feel impoverished.

The Hawaiians of old, however, and many of today, were (and are) close to the mythical dimensions of their culture. Mythology is woven into the fabric of every day. Traditionally Hawaiians have perceived a world where the personal and the archetypal levels are of a piece. They have always lived in close quarters with their gods.

What this means for many Hawaiians is that they experience every aspect of the natural landscape in at least three ways. They are keenly aware of its manifest reality, the here-and-now of the five senses; they know about the history of every detail in their environment; and they are aware of its sacred implications. They see through that veil to the mythological reality that supports the commonplace. Everything natural is also spiritual. All these experiences are woven together into a unified whole, as though they were parts of a *lei*, a garland of feathers or flowers worn to adorn life.

Although Hawaiian mythology partakes of the universality of all mythologies, it is shaped by location. Hawaiians are an island people who migrated to their islands from other islands. And island people have a unique world view. The natural elements are ever present. Pressing, expanding, in and out, like the tides, like nature itself. The nature myths of the Hawaiians have evolved in response to a particular island setting. The Hawaiians' sense of place embraces the continuum of land and sea and sky. They live on volcanoes where Pele still erupts. These are the highest and most massive structures on this planet. Hawaiians live in the middle of the largest ocean on earth, and until recently they were almost isolated there.

I think of the island on which I live as a container, bounded by the shore's circumference, the land's limitations. The primal energy held within that container is concentrated and powerful, perhaps accounting for some unique island experiences. The physical constraints caused by such limited boundaries can bring destructive conflicts or they can lead to positive transformations. The Hawaiian concept of *lōkahi*, harmony in unity, expresses a viewpoint in which like and unlike elements within nature and between people can be brought together into a harmonious new unity. The numerous means by which such accord or peace may be achieved is an integral part of Hawaiian traditions.

There is an analogy here that I believe is relevant for all of us. This earth of ours has become an island. Smaller suddenly and precariously contained within our planetary atmosphere. People are pressed together ever more tightly, as our use of the earth's resources increases. And we are further limited by ignorance and greed. We have lost our sense of place in the continuum of life.

The nature myths of the Hawaiians are expressions of elemental patterns within us all. These are primordial forces that continue to exist in the innermost reaches of our being, where we are truly human and can still respond to the vitality, the surge of mana, of life itself, so that we may know ourselves and know that we are truly alive and vibrating with our own experiences. These elemental patterns belong to us whether we perceive them or not, and it is urgent that we now claim them and integrate them into a new attitude that will bring individual and global healing. As Jung stated, "Gleaming islands, indeed whole continents, can still add themselves to our modern consciousness" (1969:190).

You and I may each stand alone in the bright consciousness of daylight, the Ao, and each of us casts an individual shadow, but we can help each other when we understand how the tales of our personal histories are interconnected within the mythology of our common histories. We can search within Pō, the dark, universal source, for the roots of our common past and the seeds to our joined future. We, too, are children of the land and are brothers and sisters to all of nature.

The communal myth about the search for the water of life may point toward a modern mythology which will constellate, a myth with enough mana to become a mythology of the entire planet. Perhaps, then, all of the world's people will live in harmony with themselves, their mutual environment, and with each other. But first we must each lift the veils that cover our own eyes, individually experiencing for ourselves the mythological foundation that truly supports us.

Recently I had a conversation with an intelligent young Hawaiian woman who has reached impressive success in her chosen profession. We were talking about our modern problems as women, which include our relationships with men, with our own work, and within the larger society where we both live. We spoke of the passion newly emerging from the women around us, which was presenting men and women alike with new difficulties and few solutions. We both knew that as yet there are no clear guidelines for the resolution of our problems. The future is invisible and the roads have never been traveled before.

"We're going to have to find our own myths," the young woman said. And I agreed.

We find our own myths as we walk along our individual paths, finding our way as we move, step by step, toward wholeness. The goal itself is an impossible vision to actualize, but the journey is the way to ourselves.

> Above, above
> all birds in air
> below, below
> all earth's flowers
> inland, inland
> all forest trees
> seaward, seaward
> all ocean fish
> sing out and say
> again the refrain
> Behold this lovely world
> (Pukui and Korn 1973:193–194)

GLOSSARY OF HAWAIIAN WORDS

Akua God, goddess, spirit, ghost, devil, image, idol; also divine, supernatural, godly.

'Alae Mudhen, a black wading bird with a red frontal plate.

Ao Light, day, daylight, dawn, enlighten.

'Aumākua Family or personal gods; guardian and ancestral spirits; deified ancestors who might assume various forms, especially those of animals; sing. 'Aumakua.

Hā Breath, to breathe; spirit breathed from the mouth, life; also stalk that supports the leaf and enfolds the stem of certain plants, such as the taro.

Hula 'ula Red feather.

Kahiki Foreign, any foreign country; Tahiti.

Kahuna Priest, sorcerer, magician, minister, expert in any profession; pl. Kāhuna.

Kalo Taro.

Kama Child, person.

Kama'āina Native born; literally land child or child of the land; kama = child, 'āina = land.

Kaona Hidden meaning; concealed reference, as to a person, thing, or place; words with double meanings.

Kapu Taboo, prohibition; special privilege; sacredness; forbidden; sacred, holy, consecrated; sing. and pl.

Keiki Child, baby, youngster.

Kilu A gourd or coconut shell, used as a quoit in the game of kilu. The player chanted as he or she tossed the kilu toward an object placed in front of a person of the opposite sex; a prize of a sexual nature was collected when the object was hit by the player.

Kumu Source, beginning, base or basis, teacher, origin; also main stalk of a plant.

Mahalo   Thanks, gratitude.

Malo   A male loincloth.

Mana   Supernatural or divine power, miraculous power; powerful authority.

Moʻo   Lizard, reptile of any kind, dragon, serpent; water spirit.

ʻOhana   Family, relative, kin group, related.

Olonā   A native shrub used for making fishing nets and carrying nets.

Pāʻū   Woman's skirt, sarong.

Pō   Night, darkness, obscurity; chaos; the realm of the gods; pertaining to or of the gods.

Puaʻa   Pig, hog, swine, pork.

BIBLIOGRAPHY

Andersen, Johannes C. 1969. *Myths and Legends of the Polynesians.* Rutland, VT: Charles E. Tuttle.

Barrère, Dorothy B., Mary Kawena Pukui, and Marion Kelly. 1980. *Hula: Historical Perspectives.* Pacific Anthropological Records no. 30. Honolulu: Bishop Museum Press.

Beckwith, Martha. [1940] 1970. *Hawaiian Mythology.* Reprint. Honolulu: University of Hawaii Press.

———. [1951] 1972. *The Kumulipo.* Reprint. Honolulu: University Press of Hawaii.

Campbell, Joseph, with Bill Moyers. 1988. *The Power of Myth.* New York: Doubleday.

Charlot, John. 1983. *Chanting the Universe: Hawaiian Religious Culture.* Hong Kong and Honolulu: Emphasis International.

Colum, Padraic. [1937] 1973. *Legends of Hawaii.* Reprint. New York: Ballantine Books.

Cooper, J. C. 1978. *An Illustrated Encyclopaedia of Traditional Symbols.* London: Thames and Hudson.

Elbert, Samuel H., ed. 1959. *Selections from Fornander's Hawaiian Antiquities and Folk-lore.* Honolulu: University of Hawaii Press.

Emerson, Nathaniel B. [1909] 1964. *Unwritten Literature of Hawaii: The Sacred Songs of the Hula.* Reprint. Rutland, VT: Charles E. Tuttle.

———. [1915] 1978. *Pele and Hiiaka: A Myth from Hawaii.* Reprint. Rutland, VT: Charles E. Tuttle.

Fanua, Tupou Posesi. 1975. *Po Fananga: Folk Tales of Tonga.* San Diego: Tofua Press.

Handy, E. S. Craighill. [1927] 1985. *Polynesian Religion.* Bernice P. Bishop Museum Bulletin 34. Reprint. Millwood, NY: Kraus Reprint.

Handy, E. S. Craighill, and Mary Kawena Pukui. [1958] 1972. *The Poly-nesian Family System in Ka-'u, Hawai'i*. Reprint. Rutland, VT: Charles E. Tuttle.

Handy, E. S. Craighill, and Elizabeth Green Handy, with Mary Kawena Pukui. 1972. *Native Planters in Old Hawaii: Their Life, Lore, and Environment*. Bernice P. Bishop Museum Bulletin 233. Honolulu: Bishop Museum Press.

Harding, M. Esther. 1971. *Woman's Mysteries, Ancient and Modern*. New York: C. P. Putnam's Sons, for the C. G. Jung Foundation for Analytical Psychology.

Hillman, James. 1979. "Senex and Puer: An Aspect of the Historical and Psychological Present." In *Puer Papers*. Irving, TX: Spring Publications.

Jung, C. G. 1953–1979. *Collected Works of C. G. Jung*. 20 vols. Edited by Sir Herbert Read, Michael Fordham, Gerhard Adler, and William McGuire; translated by R. F. C. Hull. Bollingen Series 20. Princeton, NJ: Princeton University Press.

———. [1953] 1966. *Two Essays on Analytical Psychology*. Vol. 7 of *Collected Works of C. G. Jung*.

———. [1956] 1967. *Symbols of Transformation*. Vol. 5 of *Collected Works of C. G. Jung*.

———. [1959] 1968. *Archetypes and the Collected Unconscious*. Vol. 9, pt. 1 of *Collected Works of C. G. Jung*.

———. [1953] 1968. *Psychology and Alchemy*. Vol. 12 of *Collected Works of C. G. Jung*.

———. [1960] 1969. *The Structure and Dynamics of the Psyche*. Vol. 8 of *Collected Works of C. G. Jung*.

———. 1976. *The Visions Seminars*. Books 1 and 2. Zurich: Spring Publications.

Jung, C. G., and Kerényi, C. [1949] 1963. *Essays on a Science of Mythology*. Translated by R. F. C. Hull, New York: Harper and Row.

Kahiolo, G. W. 1978. *He Moolelo No Kamapuaa: The Story of Kama-puaa*. Translated by Esther T. Mookini and Erin C. Neizmen, with David Tom. Honolulu: Hawaiian Studies Program, University of Hawaii.

Kanahele, George S. 1986. *Kū Kanaka, Stand Tall*. Honolulu: University of Hawaii Press and Waiaha Foundation.

Kapiikauinamoku. 4 March 1956. "Song of Eternity, The Courtship of Wakea." *The Honolulu Advertiser*.

Leach, Maria, ed. 1949. *Standard Dictionary of Folklore, Mythology, and Legend.* 2 vols. New York: Funk and Wagnalls.

Luomala, Katharine. [1949] 1971. *Maui-of-a-Thousand-Tricks: His Oceanic and European Biographers.* Bernice P. Bishop Museum Bulletin 198. Reprint. New York: Kraus Reprint.

———. [1951] 1971. *The Menehune of Polynesia and Other Little People of Oceania.* Bernice P. Bishop Museum Bulletin 203. Reprint. New York: Kraus Reprint.

———. [1955] 1986. *Voices on the Wind: Polynesian Myths and Chants.* Honolulu: Bishop Museum Press.

McBride, L. R. 1972. *The Kahuna: Versatile Mystics of Old Hawaii.* Hilo, HI: Petroglyph Press.

Neumann, Erich. [1955] 1963. *The Great Mother: An Analysis of the Archetype.* Translated by Ralph Manheim. Princeton, NJ: Princeton University Press.

———. 1973. "The Moon and Matriarchal Consciousness." In *Fathers and Mothers,* edited by Patricia Berry. Zurich: Spring Publications.

Pogue, John F. 1978. *Moolelo of Ancient Hawaii.* Translated by Charles W. Kenn. Honolulu: Topgallant Publishing.

Poignant, Roslyn. 1967. *The Myths of Polynesia, Micronesia, Melanesia, Australia.* London: Paul Hamlyn.

Pukui, Mary Kawena. 1983. *'Ōlelo No'eau: Hawaiian Proverbs and Poetical Sayings.* Bernice P. Bishop Museum Special Publication 71. Honolulu.

Pukui, Mary Kawena, and Samuel H. Elbert. 1971. *Hawaiian Dictionary.* Honolulu: University Press of Hawaii.

———. 1986. *Hawaiian Dictionary.* Rev. ed. Honolulu: University of Hawaii Press.

Pukui, Mary Kawena, E. W. Haertig, and Catherine A. Lee. 1972. *Nānā i ke Kumu* (Look to the source). Honolulu: Hui Hanai.

Pukui, Mary Kawena, and Alfons L. Korn. 1973. *The Echo of Our Song: Chants and Poems of the Hawaiians.* Honolulu: University Press of Hawaii.

Pukui, Mary Kawena, Samuel H. Elbert, and Esther T. Mookini. 1974. *Place Names of Hawaii.* Rev. ed. Honolulu: University Press of Hawaii.

Reed, A. W. 1963. *Treasury of Maori Folklore.* Wellington, NZ: A. H. and A. W. Reed.

Sanford, John A. 1974. In *He!*, by Robert A. Johnson. King of Prussia, Pa.: Religious Publishing Co.

von Franz, Marie-Louise. 1972. *Patterns of Creativity Mirrored in Creation Myths*. Zurich: Spring Publications.

Walker, Barbara G. 1983. *The Woman's Encyclopedia of Myths and Secrets*. San Francisco: Harper and Row.

Westervelt, W. D. 1910. *Legends of Maui—a demi god of Polynesia, and of his mother Hina*. Honolulu: Hawaiian Gazette.

———. [1916] 1963a. *Hawaiian Legends of Ghosts and Ghost-Gods*. Reprint. Rutland, VT: Charles E. Tuttle.

———. [1916] 1963b. *Hawaiian Legends of Volcanoes*. Reprint. Rutland, VT: Charles E. Tuttle.

Whitmont, Edward C. 1984. *Return of the Goddess*. New York: Crossroads Publishing.

Woods, Ralph Louis, and Herbert B. Greenhouse, eds. 1974. *The New World of Dreams*. New York: Macmillan.

INDEX